A Promise

From

the Heart

by
Wendy Ellis

A Promise From the Heart

For permissions contact:
wendyellisbooks@gmail.com

www.wendyellisbooks.com

ISBN: 978-0692737750

First Edition
Printed in the United States of America

Published by
Nike Star Publishing

Share a young woman's life as she seeks A Promise From the Heart. The real life drama takes you on Joanna Styles's journey to find love after an accident takes her family from her. She leaves her university professorship to pursue her career as a neonatal nurse in the Intensive Care Unit saving baby's lives. While the women nurses and friends around her become engaged and pregnant, Joanna, the only survivor of her family, dates, hikes and volunteers at the botanical gardens. Hoping for more, she struggles against modern day realities to create what many of us have taken for granted, a family of her own.

Brad Walters, is a young businessman has traveled abroad learning international business skills and he rises in his company. Joanna sees him as the sincere, ideal man, and he becomes the companion she leans on since her parent's death. Brad's commitment to work cannot be confused with the commitment to love.

Sara, a neighbor and best friend to Joanna is a soccer mom and PTA member with three children, a husband, sisters, nieces, and nephews. In their friendship, Joanna and Sara share the womanly pursuit of happiness in the suburbs, but while Joanna seeks to fill her life with family, Sara is a bit overwhelmed wishing only for a few moments to herself.

Moving from her familiar home on Troon Mountain to another state Joanna creates a new life at the beach. Meeting new friends she gains more confidence, learns to sail, and the surprise of a lifetime awaits her here. Will Brad follow thru on his promise? Will faith make her dream reality?

The novel, A Promise From the Heart, touches your heart. It captures the thrill and heartbreak of life, love and romance and has you laughing and crying with her.

Spain the Accident

*I*n the restaurant of the elegant hotel, several businessmen raised their glasses to another toast as the waiter removed dishes from the dining table. The room was grandly decorated with reds and gold. This afternoon meeting was to confirm and share the success that they had achieved. Dining on shrimp, roasted beef, cheeses, bread and many vegetable dishes each uniquely prepared, everyone had eaten well. The wine was also severed and consumed generously. One man raised his glass and the others followed. "La Vida. Saluda, Amigos!" The meeting was a celebration and everyone was in great spirits. As they left the table, three of the men in dark suits headed down a long corridor within the hotel toward their rooms, while most of the others went to the lobby and waited for their cars to be brought around by the valet.

Standing by the fountain that poured water from the many lion's heads carved in stone were two men from the group. A tall well-built man with dark hair not yet 30, the youngest of the businessmen, shook hands with an older stout gentleman with a mustache. "Thank you, ah, Gracias," he said eagerly. They hugged each other with a brief firm pat around the back and shoulder first to the left and then to the right.

"Llama a mi manana y nosotros hablamos". (Call me tomorrow and we will talk.)

The valet opened the door to the young man's black Carrera and he stepped in. "Adios mi bien hombre. Manana."

Out of the rearview mirror, the spires and towers of the old Spanish hotel faded away in the background as the Carrera quickly reached top speed on highway 220 toward the Costa Del Sol. The young man reached for his cell phone. Listening to his messages with one hand holding the phone, he reached for a cigarette with the other hand while his knee held the steering wheel steady.

"Ah Carlos", he said under his breath as he listened to his messages and laughed heartily. And then "Loco!" he hollered loudly as he swerved around another driver almost dropping his now lit cigarette. He pulled the wheel hard and let the phone fly in the air trying to correct his first turn while he looked back around to see the other driver waving his hand fiercely. Then at the same time something in the road threw the car, there was a loud bang and the Carrera tipped up and over the center divider sending it air born into oncoming traffic. His only thought was "NO" holding tightly to the wheel everything went black.

There was a series of bangs, and squealing tires and then one loud smash as the car settled on top of the front hood of an oncoming vehicle breaking the windshield. It was a tourist's rented car. The noise of breaking glass shattered the late afternoon hum of traffic. Cars stopped, and people gathered around the crash site. A series of smaller accidents surrounded

7

the three major vehicles. Someone called for the policia and the medicales and soon sirens were heard in the distance becoming louder as they approached.

The young businessman was removed from his car his athletic, toned and firm body was now limp with blood streaming from his head. The couple, tourists, in the rental car, were also badly injured, and after being extracted from the wreckage, they were taken immediately by ambulance to the hospital. Two adults and one child were taken from the cars that had been following the rental car. One woman had a broken leg and another had cuts and complaints of pain.

The policia took over traffic control. Cones were set up to section off the crash site while the drivers were whistled to and waved at by the white-gloved officers working to clear the traffic on the highway. Tow trucks and street sweepers arrived performing their jobs and left the scene.

Several hours passed and the highway resumed to its normal hum of traffic. The setting sun drew streaks of color across the European sky and the spires and rooftops of buildings were becoming golden. Soon the sky would grow darker as it did each night but tonight several lives would be forever changed.

Summer a Time for Love

Four Years Later

*T*hey sat on top of the hillside on a large rock, a homemade quilt spread across the hard ground. The evening sky was glowing with the last streaks of orange and red, which were disappearing behind the mountains in the country town of Cave Creek, Arizona. They had arrived early and climbed up the little town's mountain landscape to this peak. As it grew darker the stars began to appear.

Joanna Styles sat on the quilt with her boyfriend Brad beside her. She was a lean and long-legged young woman with blonde dangling hair. The angles of her face were softened in the early moonlight. Wearing denim shorts and a red silk top she glowed a simple beauty. Leaning back she beamed at Brad and then closed her eyes vowing to remember every detail. She was feeling very happy. It was the kind of magical night when love blossoms. Everything was perfect, she thought.

Brad stood up; his silhouette was outlined by the sky becoming all twinkly with stars. It was a beautiful night. "Show me the little dipper?" Joanna asked and "Will you show me, Aaron, again?" she asked without giving him a chance to reply. Brad had extensively studied the heavens. Having spent many hours flying planes it was not surprising to Joanna that Brad knew all about the constellations as well. She found it romantic.

"Look across here," he pointed. "See how the two connect here and then up and over to the left..." He swept his arm and drew the imaginary figure.

"Oh, there I see!" Joanna exclaimed. Nights like this seemed to make up for those Saturdays and weekday evenings when he was busy. "I've things to do at the hanger," he would say.

"Oh," Joanna would reply quickly, as she always did in this situation, "I've got a million things to do."

They found the little dipper, big dipper, Great Bear, and Venus as one by one the constellations came out as the sky continued to grow darker. In the valley below, the main street, which had about four restaurant-saloons, one gas station, and a cluster of gift shops, was jammed with cars. The shop's signs and headlights of the cars shown red and yellow and white. There was an echo of hootin' and hollering and a Mexican radio station could be heard with its mariachi music now and then in the distance.

Couples and families were walking along the side of the road. Every so often, a car would drive in on the dirt road below them circle around and drive off. A pickup truck pulled off to the side of the road, parked next to the older home and a young couple jumped out and sat on the flatbed of their truck, their stereo playing an old Dave Mason song. It was the fourth of July. People had come from around the valley to the little town and gathered together to see the annual fireworks.

"We oughta climb down now. Jo?" Brad was saying. It was his main thought the last little while and it kept resurfacing. "Maybe when the fireworks start we could start down at least they would light the ground for a little bit more. We could take a few steps at a time."

"I don't think it's going to get any darker, Brad. If we have to climb down we may as well wait until after, we have the perfect spot!" Over the last few months, she had begun to see how much time he was preoccupied with something. It takes away from our fun she thought to herself. Here we are on top of a mountain with our own special view away from the crowd. The night air had cooled to a comfortable 79 degrees from the 102-degree day. There was an ever so slight breeze and she felt at peace.

"It was a pretty steep climb, especially by that ridge. We'll have to watch out for the jumping cactus. If we go off to the left of this rock and around that boulder..." He was standing again and pointing into the distance. Joanna, from her spot on the quilt, was noticing his arms strong and lightly tanned. His dark hair was short and told all that met him that he was a career man in the business world, clean cut hard working, and honest. He had a kind yet serious face with a cleft chin, his shoulders were sturdy and he carried his six feet two inches well. His dark metal- framed aviator style sunglasses that reminded Jo of his hobby with planes and flying were now neatly folded in their case on the blanket.

Joanna was sprawled out face up to the sky on the quilt. "Come here," she called.

His eyes sparkled in response. She was a modest woman unaware of her beauty. She just wanted to have fun.

Her mother and father had passed away in a car crash a few years ago years ago. Now at age 30 she had become as independent as a young woman can, always feeling like she had to do something more, not that her parents had set impossible standards.

Her mother worked in a medical office as a receptionist and her father was a University professor of psychology. His profession made for an interesting family life as every current event could be analyzed as to its roots and causes, thus seen in an entirely different perspective. Joseph Styles was not the head of the department but he had planned to be eventually. His calm laid-back manner may have hidden his desire for advancement. At University functions, it was Joanna's mother, Celeste, who was outspoken. She was intelligent, informed and excited about being out and about in the world. Together, her parents made a good couple.

Joanna had taken advantage of her tuition benefit provided by her father's employment and had earned two undergraduate degrees. She loved the college atmosphere and was intrigued by many subjects. Having a double major, her first degree was in geology and psychology. She earned a graduate degree in geology and became an assistant professor. After her parent's death, the University had become like an extended home to her and so staying on to study more sciences in anatomy and physiology and earn her nursing degree was almost therapeutic.

In some ways, Joanna was more like her mother. Celeste was a strong woman she spoke her mind but gently but firmly. Having many interests, she had many activities and friends. There was a church group, the PTA, lunches with her friends from the office, and University functions she attended with her husband. Celeste had quit her job in the medical office after having married Joseph and having Joanna, but she felt like she was missing something not working and returned to the medical office part time. Joanna was an only child. Joanna and Celeste had the best of both worlds. Celeste had plenty of time to work, to be out socially, and time to take Joanna to dance recitals, the park and the zoo, Joanna's favorite. And as time went on and Joanna grew to a young woman, the two continued their mother-daughter events of shopping, lunches, and even weekend vacations.

Joanna, early on at age 22, had become a student professor in the geology department. Later, that association with the University plus the money from her parent's passing allowed her to go on as a student and earn her degree in Nursing. Having seen her parents in the ICU their last few days she developed a kind of a love, no, a need to be in medicine and to help people. When she graduated she went to the hospital and began working in the nursery and the neonatal intensive care unit (the NICU). The hospital became her anchor in life now that her family was gone.

"The nursery is where all life starts' she thought, one day while doing her university internship. She had often wondered as a child what it would've been like to have a brother or a sister. Now for the last three years, the hospital was the new home of her work. She loved her work. She moved out of the university town of Tempe to the outer suburbs of northern Scottsdale. Life's consequences had afforded her a nice 3,000 square foot house with a yard and a pool. Owning land and a home made her feel like she belonged in this world. She now made the 45-minute drive into downtown to go to work her 2-3 shifts a week. Joanna settled into her new life with new friends at the hospital and a home and garden to maintain. She had dated residents, someone from public relations, and friends of friends, hoping to have a husband and a family of her own.

Meeting Brad was the result of high tech dating she called it, where singles wrote an ad in the University paper leaving a box e-mail address. She answered Brad's ad and they chatted so well they decided to meet at a popular restaurant downtown. Hence, when anyone asked where they met Brad would say at the restaurant and Joanna would say the University. Then they would laugh! Brad in his 30s was a few years older than Joanna. His connection to the university was that he had worked in the financial aid offices early in his career and he still received the University newsletter and other publications. After leaving the

14

University position he spent some time abroad in Europe working in business and seeing the world before going on to work for a firm in downtown Scottsdale.

The last 9 months Brad and Joanna were steady. Summer cookouts, fall hikes, and Christmas parties had brought them to this Fourth of July night. They had made love for the first time just days before Christmas Eve. After a holiday party, they had returned to Joanna's house. As they sat reviewing the fun filled evening of gift giving, friends, food and drinks their laughter and talk turned to passion. As they kissed, they pressed their bodies close. Her velvet dress he unzipped easily and soon it fell to the floor. Moments later their clothes lay tangled as were their bodies while they discovered each other for the first time. As they lay together through the night he wrapped his arms around her and told her stories of flying through the clouds and landing on narrow runways on top mountain plateaus in the desert. She listened intensely imagining the sky and the mountaintops, and the danger and excitement all mixed together. They fell asleep with Joanna on his shoulder where she slept all through the night. It was a night that brought them both the surrender and the closeness of love.

"Hey, Jo climb down?" Brad's voice brought her attention out of her daydream to gaze on him. He crouched beside her looking east.

"Oh look they're starting!" Off in the distance, the rockets whistled skyward and exploded red and green and blue little stars. As they scattered outward her heart lightened. One with little yellow dots became long curved lines like a blossoming flower. Another one became a smiley face made of a circle of green dots with two blue dots for eyes and a red curved mouth. It appeared bright and shiny and then faded away. There were also red hearts, now stars now sparkle with pops and thunderous booms. They lay with their heads together turning their chins as they attempted to see the face or the design that formed from each shower of stars. Sometimes they sat up, sometimes they interlocked arms and sometimes they leaned on their elbows. They pointed and oohed and awed as did the crowd below. At the grand finale, multiple rockets shot upward filling the sky bursting with color to the music of the Star Spangled Banner.

Climbing down was not the chore Brad had expected. Joann took his outreached hand a couple times and once she leaned on his shoulder as she jumped dismounting from a rocky ledge. They drove home with quiet talk and saw more fireworks over the horizon in the city below.

"It was a perfect night, Jo," Brad said.

"Yes," she replied dreamily.

"You know I want you to be happy and to go out and do things." His voice wandered off.

"I do," Joanna replied almost defensively. He was always putting up the wall, the line of separation, where she had her activities and he had his.

"I'll be going to the hanger Saturday. The journal is almost complete. We're sending it to the publisher next Monday. It's been a lot of work Jo. I appreciate your working around my schedule but there's more Jo." He continued. "It's just that you need to realize.... well we're good Jo, good friends...."

"And that's all we need." Joanna finished his sentence, not wanting to hear more not wanting to be put off by him as he did every so often.

"But I'm not thinking of the future."

Joanna had heard these words before. "You can't count on the future Brad," Joanna implored. Outwardly, she seemed to always live fully in the present tense as if denying herself a future, but in her heart, she wanted more. She forced herself to be patient to live in the present and accept every blessing every day offered. "What we have is now, today. Tomorrow I could...."

He interrupted her knowing that this was coming from her parents having died young. Jo didn't talk about it or what happened except that it was a car accident that ended their lives. All she would say is how she missed them. "Jo you're a great girl and you deserve better. You want to have a family and I'm just not there now." Joanna silently looked away. She never talked about her family of lack of it. She was not going to let him make her sad. Every few dates, he went on to the future. Things were going fine now, so why was he so ah... she couldn't find a word to complete her thought.

"Bra...aad," she whined as she moved closer. "You're my bud." She peered up at him and fluttered her lashes. He put his hand on hers and they soon arrived at Jo's house.

Kissing goodnight in the hallway he unwrapped her festive scarf from her neck, one her mother had given her, and he kissed her neck before placing the scarf on the hall table. They kissed in the hallway their bodies close, he breathed deep and stood back now his full height. "Good night now go to bed you're working in the morning." He was as disciplined with her as he was with himself.

"Bye," She replied keeping the mood light. He smiled as he left closing the door gently. The next day was Sunday and she was on for the hospital's standard 12-hour shift starting 7 a.m. in the NICU.

Joanna lay awake that evening. The frustration that she felt grew into anger and hurt, all of which had grown out of the relationship in the last few months. She turned over and over stuffing pillows all around her. 'Friends' she thought, of course, they were good friends. Friendship makes the foundation for a lasting relationship. Why must he deny the true love they have?

She thought back on last Christmas when they first made love, and of the passing Spring when they hiked Camelback, Piestewa, and Pinnacle Peaks. She recalled the Society of the Arts Fund Raising Formal they attended at the end of May. At the party, he had said she seemed like the perfect girlfriend, " beautiful and she hikes too!" Over the last six months, since Christmas, they had shared long intimate late night talks and lovemaking both light and easy. All the while the echo of his words tonight haunted her "just friends... no future... not a future with you ...."

Words, more words.... She tried to block them out to sleep, as she needed to be alert the next day. She changed her focus on to her dream, the dream she kept to herself and held on tight to somewhere in the back of her mind. It was her future when she would know a promise from the heart and her life would be filled with happy times- a wedding, children, family outings, holiday and anniversary celebrations, daily dinners together and making love.

She smiled at him as he stood handsomely in his black suit and her in a flowing gown as they exchanged golden bands. Flowers adorned the walkways and all their friends were gathered in attendance. The feeling was that of excitement, anticipation, and satisfaction, longing and loving all in one. "I cherish you and every day with you," he would say and with that she was off to sleep in another world that exists only when you are sleeping

The Unit

orking in the NICU was pretty routine after two years. Arriving at about 10 to 15 minutes of the hour she'd wait with the other nurses in the hallway for the assignment to be issued. After getting the day's assignment the nurses went through the double doors to scrub in before going to find their babies in the rows of isolettes that filled the large room. At the scrub sink, everyone would chat about things... Mary's new babysitter, Susan's date last night, Becky's child's grades, the new admissions to the nursery, the residents were forming a basketball team....

This year when Lisa became engaged, Mary had her first child and Barb got married, Joanna was beginning to realize that almost all her friends were getting married and becoming mothers. If Brad would stop worrying and just enjoy our time together everything will fall into place for them, she thought. For now, she worked at finding some new single friends to go out with and she did. Of all the nurses, the traveler nurses were especially interested in running about town to see everything from parks to plays. She had gone with them on lots of adventures like mountain hiking and river kayaking.

At the bedside of her assigned baby's isolette, Joanna received a report on her patient's condition. She'd have either two or three babies to care for that day. Heart and respiratory monitors alarming frequently around her, nurses calling codes overhead, doctors and surgeons rushing about, and parents in tears were all part of Joanna's day at work. Joanna was strong like her mother and sensitive like her father. She made a good nurse.

One of her patients was a "32 weeker". The baby was born 32 weeks into the pregnancy. She was in an oxygen hood and getting respiratory treatments every 4 hours. The baby wasn't eating yet and so she had an IV line. The mother came to the unit in her pajamas and robe. "There are so many wires," the mother said peering into the isolette at her baby. "I hope she will be out of the oxygen soon."

"Thirty-two weeks of gestation is pretty good Mrs. Santos," Joanna replied. "Her lungs are much more developed than if you would have had her earlier. It is good that the doctors were able to help you delay labor the extra few weeks until you reached the steroid window. Your little girl will eventually be weaned off the oxygen. The neonatologist said that tomorrow she should be able to start little feedings maybe 5 ccs." They went on to talk about feeding and the importance of pumping breast milk and nursing. Then Joanna carefully took the baby from the isolette separating the wires and folding them into the blanket she wrapped the baby in. She placed the baby in the mother's arms and set an oxygen mask across the baby's chest. "She's beautiful.

Bonita, and you hold her well, muy bien, Mrs. Santos," Joanna smiled as she spoke her little bit of Spanish.

"Joanna admit team to bed 17," the voice came over her bedside speaker. It was Hilda from the front desk.

"Bed 17," Joanna repeated quickly. "OK." Joanna briefed the other nurse in her row on her babies' conditions so she could watch over them while Joanna was gone. "Mrs. Santos is holding her baby. She's on blow by (oxygen) can you put her back in when she's ready? My other baby is the 28 weeker on a vent. He's not due for a treatment until nine o'clock but watch him for desats. OK, I'm going," and she rushed off.

At space 17 the four nurses gathered along with the neonatologist and Diana, the NNP, (neonatal nurse practitioner). "We're putting in lines, oxygen at 100% blow by and see how she sats, while we order oxygen pressure prongs. I want cultures and blood gasses stat," the NNP ordered the nurses. She was talking and writing at the same time.

Kelly held the O-2 mask while Joanna leaned into the speaker pressing it with her hand to call for respiratory. "I need positive pressure O-2 prongs at bed 17," she shouted into the intercom. While holding the oxygen mask with one hand Kelly comforted the baby with the other. Then she checked the over-bed warmer.

Joanna cradled the baby's feet and legs while she attached the chest leads for the cardiorespiratory monitor to the baby's tiny chest. She watched her intently as the baby gasped for breath. The women rushing about the little infant were little a ticking clock each one with their part in sync with the other. She flipped on the monitor and checked for the pattern. "Heart rate 120," she called out.

Terry was helping the NNP. Leaning over her, Terry read Diana's writing in the chart. "Jo" she called out, "D10 with sodium & potassium, and get the amp and gent."

Joanna had been setting the monitor configurations while Kelly gave another listen to the baby's chest. "Breath sounds are now equal," she announced.

To Terry, Joanna asked, "3 and 2?"

"Yes 3 and 2," Terry replied. Joanna mixed the IV fluid adding exactly 3 mEq (milliequivalents) of sodium and 2 mEq of potassium per the 100 milliliters of D10W solution. She hung the bag and connected it to the tubing which she then began feeding through the chambers of an infusion pump. She purged the lines and laid them on the counter ready for use being careful to keep the ends sterile. Then she walked to the end of the big room where the IV supplies were kept in an another room to get heparin for the arterial line, and to the unit pharmacy to get the antibiotic medications ampicillin and gentamicin.

Meanwhile, Terry had unwrapped sterile gloves for the NNP who would place the IV central lines into the veins of the baby's umbilical cord. "Sats 91," Kelly called out, "and respiratory is on its way." Terry again listened to the baby's chest with her stethoscope for a few minutes and then held the baby still while the lines were placed.

"We'll see if we can get by with prongs at 85 %," Diana said.

Terry drew out a few drops of blood which she placed into small micro collection tubes from the lines that were placed by Diana. Terry injected some of the blood into the culture tubes, set the glucose monitor up and filled more tubes for the blood chemistry panel attaching a label to each container verifying the baby's name and number.

"Heart rate's dropping," called Kelly as she re-sealed the oxygen mask and pressed in a few puffs of oxygen over the baby's face, rubbed the baby's shoulder and flicked her fingers on the baby's limp feet.

"Almost done here," Diana replied quietly, calmly and confidently as she listened to the baby's heart.

Returning from the pharmacy Joanna squeezed in closer having seen the monitor, she ducked down and checked below the bed where the oxygen line was coming from to verify the settings on the wall. "you're at 100%," she called out as she raised up from her crouched position and placed the medications she was holding on the counter.

Diana had finished the line placement and was working on her examination of the newborn. Terry paused a moment having finished preparing the blood samples that were to go to the lab. Kelly rubbed the baby's shoulders and cradled the baby's body. Joanna stood at the counter drawing the exact dose of each antibiotic out of the vials. She watched the monitor. "Coming up," Joanna called out, "74...76...89".

"Good. Let's get this x-ray done and the IV fluid going," Diana said.

"X-ray," a gal called out as she approached the bed with portable machine rolling through the unit on wheels like a tractor. Joanna wrapped the hard metal framed x-ray sheet with a baby blanket and placed it under the infant while Terry held the baby up ever so carefully. Then everyone cleared the space for only a moment while the picture was done. Terry went on to assess the baby's head, eyes, ears, nose, shoulders, chest, abdomen, groin and hips, feet and all while she verbalized her observations, Joanna wrote them on the chart and she did this in just minutes. Virginia checked the meds that Joanna had drawn up and labeled for absolute accuracy before placing them on the counter for use. Virginia went to send the blood samples to the hospital lab. The respiratory tech arrived and was now assessing the baby's lungs for his notes and set up the high-pressure oxygen prongs with its tubes and lines and monitor of its own.

The X-ray tech came back to say the films were ready to be seen. "I'll get Diana," Virginia said walking across the room.

Virginia came back with Diana walking a step ahead of her. "Lines are in good placement," Diana said holding up the x-ray. " Did we get the cultures sent?"

"Yes," replied Terry.

"Sent," replied Kelly.

Hilda said the nurse for the mother called over and they will be here in 15, she wants us to know her name is April." Virginia said.

"She's a cutie, how's she been sat-ing?" Diana said admiring the baby girl though the clear plastic plexiglass dome that was now her home.

"They've been 93 to 94," Terry replied.

"Good."

For one quiet moment, the five women stood over the isolette holding the little baby girl in their hearts. Silently each nurse would wish April well in her new home in the nursery. It is in this moment, this small moment, that the women acknowledge the work they did everyday saving babies' lives. Soon they would again open their awareness to the unit around them that continued to buzz with the noise of equipment and voices.

Virginia broke the silence, "I'm off to my babies," she said after she threw out the saran wraps and syringe packaging that littered the counters and she dashed off.

"OK Thanks," Terry called after her.

Terry rechecked the fluids for the ordered rate in the chart. She sneaked into the isolette to add some more soft rolled up blankets to the baby's bed, while monitoring the isolette temps, April's heart rate, respiratory rate and blood pressures on the Hewlett Packard monitor above. Together with the admitting team had settled this little one into her new home. Each nurse with their own role had played it smoothly and when they were done they dispersed throughout the unit.

"Thanks, Jo, all set now. Thanks, Kelly." Terry said.

Kelly stayed to help Terry. While Terry finished paperwork, Kelly went to get one of the units baby quilts and draped it over the isolette before taping it in place. This made for a quieter darker bed for the baby, and it decreased the noise in the room. Kelly then made out the baby's name card and also the baby's ID bands placing one on the bed and the other around the baby's ankle, and Joanna went back to her babies.

The respiratory tech, Ben, who had placed the oxygen prongs on the baby, added the oxygen monitors and also listened to the baby's lungs came back to the bedside. "Terry your baby?"

"Yah. First, admit." (admission to the NICU)

"Lucky you."

"Oh, I like being on admit team it keeps things rolling, you know?"

"You're here on traveling status. Is that right?" He said as he wrote his notes on the clipboard.

"It's my first time in Arizona and I love it. Hand me that cord," she said as she pointed across the front of him. "Thanks." She tucked in the cords around the baby before closing the isolette.

"You want to go bowling sometime?"

"Bowling?" She glared at him for a second. " I don't bowl." She said flatly.

"NICU nurses," Ben said as he shook his head and walked away.

Terry called after him, "Hey what's that about?"

Diana showed up just then. "How's she sat-ing?" meaning her oxygen saturation.
"97" Terry replied.

"Let's give her an hour then you can wean her O2 (oxygen flow) for sats keeping them about 94."

"Sounds good," Terry said as she returned her attention the counter and her charts now writing and entering into the computer all that had been done by the team of nurses.

Ben had drifted off feeling a bit rejected. But Terry was just like that, especially when at work speaking her mind in a straightforward manner.

Across the room, Joanna had walked a short distance to another row in the large room where her other patient was. He had been more of a challenge the day before dropping his heart rate, she had been told by the nurse going off shift. This morning he had been much better. "Were they good?" she said to her pod-mate nurse Sharon.

"Oh, very quiet not a beep. No decels or desats from your little guy," she said referring to the many monitors and beeping alarms. "Mrs. Santos stayed about 15 minutes then I put her baby back. She likes to be on her side."

"Oh great, Thanks, Sharon."

"How's the admit?" Sharon asked.

"She's cute, a 30 weeker with pressure oxygen prongs and lines." And with that said she focused her attention on her other baby. He was a 28 weeker on a ventilator to assist his breathing. The use of artificial lung surfactant had greatly increased his ability to be supported with ventilated oxygen. He needed hourly medications as well as respiratory treatments. His IV line was an umbilical IV line into his belly button and he had several other lines.

Off in the background, Joanna could hear "code team bed 32." She let that announcement pass as she was on admit team today, not code team. It was one more noise that caused a quiet movement of nurses and doctors as the rushed to attend to the baby at bed 32.

Joanna carefully opened her baby's isolette and repositioned him as she did with every treatment. She checked his lungs and his lines and changed his diaper. She gave him his medications via the umbilical IV line and suctioned the ET tube he breathed through. She cooed to him ever so softly and told him how he would be fine. She placed his little hands to his mouth and tucked them by his face, as well, she tucked his legs and feet up under him with soft flannel blankets rolled around them to support him like a nest. His head was the size of a big baseball, his skin pale and smooth with eyes that opened only slightly and peered at Joanna in wonder. She adored his long eyelashes and tiny fingers. His whole hand would wrap around one finger of Joanna's. She had dressed him in light blue. She chose a knit hat and a jumpsuit type outfit to help keep him warm. It had snaps that she snapped around his umbilical lines and his cardiac monitor lines. He seemed content as he closed his eyes sucking on his ET tube that connected him to his ventilator and gave him the breath of life. She held her hands around him in a cupped like fashion and quietly blessed him as she did all her babies. For a few minutes, her hands stayed in that position resting around him giving him a hug to offer him security before she closed his bed.

By five o'clock the day was winding down. The new admissions had been twins, only one of them was in Terry's charge. They were both on oxygen with umbilical lines and looking well for 30 weekers. Joanna's turn on admit team had gone smoothly. She wandered over before the end of shift report time to see how the new admit baby was. She found the new mother of the babies was visiting. They had wheeled her into the NICU on a stretcher type bed. So Joanna stepped away offering privacy now and went to take the time to finish her own paperwork.

By 7 she was exhausted. Those last two hours were always the longest. She did rounds on each of her babies one more time, cleaned the bedside counter and updated the chart's index on each. She gave the oncoming nurse report and headed home the 45-minute drive to North Scottsdale.

The next two days were much the same so by Tuesday night she was looking forward to spending time relaxing on her days off. She rarely worked 3 days in a row but on occasion if the unit was short staff or there was a holiday schedule, it was expected. She was glad she was off tomorrow so she could sleep in.

At Home in Scottsdale

*M*aking iced cappuccino in her kitchen was Joanna's new specialty. The counters of her kitchen were smooth hard granite and the floor tiled in beige stone. The granite rock gave the kitchen a natural and polished look. Joanna liked how she could put anything on it hot or cold and cut on it too. She had picked out the patterns herself when she had the house built. The tile made life easy for the company, for pets and for making meals without having to be super neat. Her kitchen windows were huge. They overlooked Troon Mountain with a view extending beyond the yard's landscape to the four peaks. The ceiling was so high she could actually stand on her counter and still be looking out the window. Once she had seen a mountain lion on the rock in the wildlife wash between her house and the neighbors.

In the far counter of the kitchen was an aquarium, the largest she could fit. She had tiger fish and angelfish and swordfish and mollies. "Good morning guys." She peered in at them and gave them their food. Bluebell swam thru the coral and Sam came to the surface. While growing up her parents thought pets were meant for the zoo so now in her own home she had as many as she could. While peering at them she made her breakfast. She took the frosty glass of cappuccino and headed toward the patio wearing only blue paisley boxer shorts cuffed their highest with the waistband rolled down about her hips and a little matching blue paisley bra top.

As she walked outside the love-birds were cooing and buzzing and she cooed back to them in their tall cage that sat by the French doors. Thru the window panes, Lady Dancer could be seen lying in the shade with Joanna's new garden tool. Dancer was a yellow Labrador retriever. A very large dog she was, yet still a puppy at 1 year. Her coat was sleek and her body lean. Her little pink tongue was visible as she panted in the heat.

"No, leave it. Bad girl," she said. Dancer dropped the tool and looked away from it. "Good, leave it," Joanna called out. She sat in her favorite chair. It was one of two metal frame lounge chairs she had bought at a church rummage sale. She had replaced the cushions with fat new bright blue ones. They were low on the ground and she leaned back holding her cup of cappuccino. She had yet to replace one of the patio end tables, which now sat in the garage. Dancer had a run in with it and shattered the glass. 'Something I should do today,' she thought. She always had a to-do list, if not written it was mental.

"What a good little girl Dancer," she cooed, as Dancer placed her head in Joanna's lap. "I love you mucho." Her ears picked up and Joanna sensed she knew how much Joanna loved her even though she yelled at her all the time. "Where's your ball

Dance?, Seek." Joanna commanded. The game of seek and retrieve went on for a good long time. All through the game she surveyed the yard and strolled through the lush green grass in her bare feet. Then getting the garden hose she selectively watered certain areas and thus began game two - get-the-water. She squirted Dancer who jumped and leaped into the spray of cool water.

At 9 a.m. it was already about 90 degrees. She lived in a desert and it was this time of year when her thoughts were of moving to what she thought would be greener pastures so to speak. She pictured herself in the mountains of Colorado skiing every weekend with always a friend to go with. On the shores of sunny California, she would be surfer girl on Saturday and sail the harbor on Sunday. She scolded herself. She had to make her future happen. It nagged at her on lazy mornings like this when she was caught between enjoying what is and planning where she thought she should be. The ultimate question was what more should I be doing with my life? After busy days in the unit, it was a big change to have time to linger about, to have a sense of life outside the hospital.

I'm free Joanna thought to herself. I have no responsibility to anyone but myself, to any life but my dog and my bird and not to any bank except for a tiny mortgage. (Joanna, having been raised very responsible had put a down payment on the house that covered most of the cost of it.) I have the opportunity! So much opportunity, yet somehow I've settled here in Arizona.

"You have too much time off," her friend Sara would say. "That's your problem." After her first year in the NICU Joanna had earned the ability to go to unit reserve staff status and to set her own hours. As reserve staff, she got all the shifts she wanted. Now going on three years Joanna usually worked two or three days a week finding the stress of saving lives and the 12-hour shift plus almost 2 hour drive time a long enough day to warrant a few days off. Sara who lived two streets over, she had three children, a lawyer husband, a part-time office job, a house, a boat, a pool and brothers and sisters not to forget the sisters in law and the brothers in law and their children all of whom lived in town.

The ringing phone brought her to the present. She answered it and it was Sara. "Mary Kelly has company and wants us to come over this Saturday. Good thing. Are you off? She wants you to meet him. I only met him once...." Sara was saying. "I thought he was nice looking. Come on it will be fun. You never know, you could hit it off. I'm bringing Janie and Tracy. They are going to Greasewood Flats and I think they'll ask you to join them. You said, you had nothing to do."

"Besides, prepare a lecture I'm giving for my botanical garden day. Did you know it takes 100 yrs for the saguaro cactus to bloom one arm?" Joanna replied.

"Nurse and volunteer wildlife ranger, what a combo Jo," Sara mocked her.

"Hey, you have to admit you love the jazz nights in the garden and the kids..."

"I was kidding, just kidding. So Saturday afternoon?"

Somewhere in her intuition, Joanna knew Brad was not going to call to make plans for this weekend as he was in his not-thinking-about-the-future-let's be friends mode but still she was slow to accept the invitation.

"But Brad...." Joanna started to say.

"Forget Brad, you're not married to him," Sara jumped in.

"Is it a party?" Joanna asked Sara.

Mary Kelly was an artist and she lived right in Joanna's neighborhood. Mary Kelly's husband, Manny, handled the business end of setting up art shows and gallery openings. They had two children one went to school with Sara's daughter. It seems once they had met they would run into each other often. When Joanna was walking Dancer, Mary Kelly was going to pick up her children at school. One morning Joanna sat in Mary Kelly's studio talking about art. Soon they were talking about friendships and family and boyfriends and husbands. It seemed as if they had known each other a long time. Joanna left that day with a loaf of homemade bread and a signed print.

"No just come over to my house and then we'll stop in." Sara was saying.

The afternoon sun beamed down on Mary Kelly's backyard on Saturday afternoon. "It sure is nice weather here," Andy said. "And the sky is so blue."

"Nice?" Joanna questioned. "This is nice?"

Manny got up from his poolside chair to check the outdoor thermometer. "It's 108".

"Sure beats hot and smoggy LA. This feels more like summer, like a vacation."

Joanna looked up appreciating the sky, it was vast and she could see forever across the desert. Her feet dangled in the pool. As the adults talked poolside, Mary Kelly's girl Ellie and Sara's girl were romping in the water with floats.

Andy was a photographer, one of Manny's clients. He covered sports and did some artistic freelancing also. Wearing a T-shirt that buttoned below the neck and casual shorts, he used his hands as he talked about the team shots, the image, the decisive moment, he motioned as if to frame an action shot and then smiled at Joanna. He worked from all angles to get the action shots he took with different types equipment. As he spoke, Joanna studied him, deciding what he was all about.

While Andy's gaze was in the opposite direction the little girls had sneaked up on him. Joanna was not about to rat them out. And swoosh the little girls splashed and at tugged him and over he went in the water, shorts T-shirt and all. Everyone was laughing and he was now soaking wet and chasing the girls. Janie, Sara's girl, had his sunglasses and was trying them on showing off her new look while

Mary Kelly's girl was on the move with Andy a stroke behind her. Andy was a great sport and seemed to be enjoying all the attention. They were doing rocket dives now. Balancing one girl on his knee he would spring them out of the water into the air like a rocket.

One by one o'clock everyone changed into swimwear and was enjoying the pool. Mary Kelly went into the house and returned with Karla just up from her nap. Placing her on the cool decking she began toddling around in her Baby Gap sun-suit. It was pink and she wore a matching beanie with an elastic strap. Her curls framed her face and she had white sunscreen still visible on her cheeks. Holding some candies she offered them to others. Joanna had never seen her before as she had always been sleeping when she was over. Karla was at that age where she looked like a doll with big round eyes. Joanna now had a new friend and they were both sitting on the pool steps with Joanna supervising the baby's moves. Joanna then wrapped baby Karla in her arms and swam her around holding her up and Karla laughed seeming interested in everything. Something caught baby Karla's eye on the cool deck and soon they were making their way toward a pile of plastic toys. Karla reached for a toy and dunked it in the pool all the while Joanna holding her.

"We're all going up to Greasewood Flats for burgers and fireworks, Joanna and Sara will you be joining us?" Manny asked from his chair. "They're having another run at it something about surplus fireworks and their summer fest."

"You forget I have more at home," Sara said referring to her children.

It was a little while later that Joanna was sitting in the back of Mary Kelly's van. Sara let her daughter Janie come along to play with Mary Kelly's daughter, Ellie, but she herself had stayed home with her husband and her other children. The ladies and girls sat in the plush armchairs in the back of the van while the two men sat up front. Mary Kelly was clad in blue denim shorts and a denim vest both with colorful beaded detail. Joanna was dressed in khaki shorts and a blue shirt that tied about her waist and accentuated her breasts. "I love that bag," Joanna said.

Mary Kelly carried a backpack painted by another Arizona artist. "We met in Taos," she said as she pulled out a baby toy, "I just adored this and so we traded. I gave her one of my prints."

The baby sat in a car seat and seemed quite content. "You make it look so easy Joanna commented. She was thinking how someday she would have a baby.

"I keep it simple. I bring just a few things when I take her. I always have an extra outfit. People can worry too much and make themselves crazy."

Manny and Andy were talking housing prices. "This area here you are looking at a half a million for a 2 bedroom. That one over there is two million. Now we like this area to your right." The windows of the van were big and the day was still in full bloom at six o'clock. The desert sand shimmered golden brown in the sunlight. Mountains in the distance rose to meet the wide-open blue sky. A dirt road led them to the western style outdoor patio restaurant in the desert called Greasewood Flats, a favorite spot to take your out of town friends to get an authentic taste of the old West. A cluster of wooden picnic tables and a fire pit sat in front of one long very weathered building. A wooden porch bordered the front of the building where there hung many old time signs. They walked along the porch and peered into the windows to view the old time barber pole and telegraph office before entering the saloon.

Inside, the saloon was dark, the air just slightly thicker and people in casual dress were clustered around the bar ordering drinks and food. The wood and walls seemed all original purely by their age. Dollar bills hung from the low ceiling each one was tacked up along with a business card or some writing. They fluttered in the breeze made by the fans running in the old saloon. "Ewh," Joanna squealed. "Don't they look like bats?" They did, and Mary Kelly and Joanna laughed. It was Manny who drew everyone's attention to the end of the room to see one of Andy's photographs. It was a black and white photo of cowboys made to look old and worn. The photo fit the place.

Mary Kelly and Joanna were the last to move away from the photo. "Caballeros de Arizona," Joanna remarked. (Cowboys of Arizona)

"You speak Spanish Jo?" Mary Kelly said.

"Yeah a little, mi bien amiga (my best girlfriend), so does Brad. He learned while in Europe and Spain and all."

"Isn't that where...a" Mary Kelly stopped mid-sentence. Her though was about Jo's parents and what happened and it was not something she wanted to bring up.

"What? "

"Oh, a, well that's good, Spanish I mean, amiga. Hey, let's catch up." The girls turned about in the small shack and went over to the bar.

They ordered burgers, nachos and beers and stood around the bar until their number was called. Once outdoors they found a table to eat at. Mary Kelly, Joanna, Andy and Manny sat and talked with other guests. "There'll be fireworks tonight on the corner."

"Great, again I get two, Fourth of Julys," Joanna exclaimed.

"This girl," Mary Kelly commented, "always a party."

"Not true!" Joanna cried.

"Never a dull moment over here. Did she tell you she was a neonatal nurse?"

"Really?" Andy replied as he brushed his hand across her knee. "I'd like to see you in your scrubs." Andy laughed.

"You don't!" She said not finishing her sentence.

He nudged her playfully putting an arm around her back. Their attraction to each other was obvious. Eating hamburgers and drinking beer they admired the mountains, hummed to the music and talked.

After a while, Joanna, Mary Kelly, and the children got up and walked around the maze of antiques. The girls found the windmill, followed the stream to an old wheelbarrow and some sheds, one housed peacocks, another had goats. The children pet the donkeys and chased the potbelly pig that roamed freely on the grounds. Janie spied a jackrabbit and Ellie caught a toad. After following the pigs, peaking into sheds and cooing with the peacocks they made their way back by the hay bales and the old train to the picnic tables to finish their drinks. They emerged with Joanna carrying Janie and Mary Kelly carrying her baby Karla with Ellie in tow.

"Fireworks ladies?" Manny said as he drank the last of his beer. "After you." He motioned with his arm guiding the way back to the entrance.

Driving just a bit South and East they arrived at the corner where the fireworks were bright in the sky. The girls cheered to go up the ladder to the roof of the van and sit on top. Andy and Joanna sat on the wall. Once again with the night came the cool air and the glittering lights of the city off in the distance. The fireworks made a beautiful night even more enchanting. "This one's yours," Ellie called out to her dad. "Oh, yours is a good one Dad."

"Ooohh!" everyone echoed.

"This one's your mom!" Ellie called out.

"Wow."

"Andy, this one's Andy's".

Each firework had an owner and there were several.

41

Tonight they were right under them looking up as they exploded in the sky filled with little green, orange, blue and red stars. Joanna had never played this game before of naming the fireworks and she liked it. It was fun to be with a family and friends enjoying a new adventure and laughing totally in the moment.

Andy and Joanna talked quietly between their cheers. He told her how blue her eyes were and listened to stories of local hikes. They both had dogs and talked about the silly things their dogs did. Buster was Andy's German Shepard. Joanna laughed a lot. Holding her stomach she declared, "Stop, stop I can't laugh anymore."

"He does, he really does, Buster is a natural." He put his arm around her, helped her into the van and sat next to her.

They rode home with one extra passenger, Big Head Todd. Todd had the great misfortune of being caught by Ellie. He was the biggest toad that Joanna had ever seen. He was now a prisoner at her feet in a bucket, jumping hard enough to bang the wood board which covered the bucket.

They dropped Joanna off at her house. Andy walked with her down the sidewalk and waited while she opened her door. With the door ajar, Joanna looked up at Andy. Their eyes met as he stared at her and she smiled at him. Then she looked past him. He moved closer inhaling her scent. "I...a, I ...." He leaned into her and under the porch light their eyes met once again and their lips were now close. They stood still as the night. Andy reached out for her placing his arm around her waist just as Joanna broke the silence. " I had fun." She said softly as she moved toward him.

"I'm glad you came," he responded leaning forward and kissing her lightly on the lips and then as she moved toward him they kissed again. Several minutes went by. Joann looked up and it was Andy who softly said "Night". He paused before moving a step back. And then with excitement he added, "See you tomorrow," And he quickened his step toward the gate that led to the driveway and the waiting van.

"OK," Joanna called after him. "Good night."

Sunday evening came and they were all going for Pizza at The Pinnacle. They picked up Joanna in the SUV still talking about yesterday's adventures.

"How is everyone?" Joanna said taking her seat in the vehicle.

"Todd can jump around in my room," Ellie said. "He rivets at night."

"Rivets?" Joanna replied.

"Yeah, like this..." and Ellie tried to copy the sounds of Big Head Todd.

"We swam all day auntie Jo," said Janie, patting Joanna's leg as Joanna had sat next to her.

"Hi Joanna," Andy said from his seat.

"Sara is watching Karla for me." Mary Kelly added. "It's a trade-off."

"I see," Joanna replied.

"Whose hungry?" Manny asked and the two little girls hollered "Me" in unison and Andy chimed in as well.

At The Pinnacle, they chose a round table inside. "I'm sitting next to Joanna," Ellie said as she took her hand as children like to. Mary Kelly sat on the other side of her daughter with Janie next to her and then Manny leaving Andy to be next to Jo.

"I guess then I'll take the other side," Andy called.

They ordered 3 pizzas. "All cheese mommy, cheese," Ellie added.

Why didn't you come over swimming with us today Jo?"

"Oh I had some things to do"

"Do you know I can do cannon balls?"

"You can!" Jo replied, and the conversation went to pool games and the fun they had been having since their friend had arrived.

"Andy took pictures of the girls in the pool," Mary Kelly said to Joanna. "They are going to be quite good. If I get the right one I'm going to have it blown up life size and do a cut-out. Maybe we'll put it on Janie's wall in her room. I have all these ideas. We could do cut outs of the both of them for my parents for a gift. You know they stand up life like and all. What do you think Joann?"

"Sounds great, like in a movie I saw they cut out the children's figures life size."

"Yeah, that's what I mean."

"I'd like one of the Dancer, or maybe a cat," Joanna laughed.

"I can arrange that," Andy said.

"I was kidding."

They finished their pizzas and the girls wanted to play the games. "Why don't you two go walk outside, the garden is beautiful. Joanna will tell you about the cactus and plants,"

Mary Kelly said. She turned toward Joanna, "Hey go, go."

Out in the courtyard was a path that went around the building and into a small preserve. The cactus each had little signs naming them. Joanna and Andy strolled in the coolness of the evening, she talked about the different plants and asked him about photography and he held her hand as they walked. "Sometimes I get lonely. Lonely for a relationship with someone real like you." Andy said to her.

He stopped and looked in her eyes for just a moment. She returned the look studying his face to learn more and then looked away as the two continued to walk. "It seems like it takes forever to meet someone you like and you think you know what that person is all about and then you get to know them and it's all different than what you thought." He stopped in front of another plant. "I like this one. Does it really jump?"

"Yes and one time when I first saw them I swung my sleeve at it to see it jump and it stuck to my sleeve. I couldn't get it off. Dancer has had run-ins with them too."

"I bet that was painful."

"Yeah for both of us. You are really sweet... and you seem to enjoy the girls," Joanna said.

"I love kids and someday I'm going to have a bunch of them. Buster likes kids too. He keeps asking for a boy."

Joanna laughed. "Dancer wants one too."

"I wish you lived closer Joanna, would you visit me in LA?"

"I, well, maybe sometime. I'm sure you'll be back to see Manny. You know I have had a relationship for a while." Joanna had not thought seriously about dating, she still had hope for Brad.

"Oh. No, Manny didn't say so. Is it serious?"

"Well, I am out tonight so not really. I guess it's like you say about thinking you know someone and then not being sure you know them. Maybe you get along really good but you want different things."

"And you want different things than he?"

"I'm still figuring that out."

"Well Joanna, a girl like you, why not just ask?"

"Sometimes I think he doesn't know what he wants." She paused as they walked along the dirt path. "And then I like to see with my own eyes, to let things unfold as they will and not well,... I don't know. You can't count on your tomorrows anyway only your hope."

"Well, I hope I see you again." His hand touched hers again and the electricity they'd shared was there. She smiled. He put his arm behind her and with his hand felt the small of her back. As he pulled her close to him their lips met and as they kissed they moved closer to one another. Her lips full and soft nestled between his and her arms long and slender hugged either side of his body. As he kissed her, she squeezed the arms that held her. Feeling his well-developed muscles beneath his shirt sent flutters through her body. She was breathless when they heard a voice.

"Hey there!" It was Manny and the family in the distance. "Are you enjoying the desert?" He said as he came closer. Joanna and Andy walked across the dirt path to met Manny by the fence.

"This area is a really a nice touch. I like the design."

"Big change from L.A. hey Andy? We're ready to head back."

"OK then."

They drove back stopping at Joanna's house first. Andy got out and walked Joanna to the door. "Good night," he said with a smile, giving her kiss and a hug.

"See you around it was nice." Joanna thought it was nice as she closed the door and leaned back against it stopping to gather her thoughts. He knows what he wants and says it. It's right there, she thought and she liked that. Joann called to her dog. "Dance?"

Joanna worked the next day (which was Monday) and it was the reason why she had to go in the minute they got back that night. Never did she ask how long he was staying. The day after on Tuesday however she had the perfect excuse to stop in Mary Kelly's and that was to see how Big Head Todd was doing. To her dismay, Andy and Todd were both gone. Todd had been returned home to Greasewood earlier that day by dad Manny, and Andy went back to California.

"Still he was the biggest darn toad I'd ever seen," Joanna said laughing.

"And, I'm sure you had your share of toads" Mary Kelly added.

They laughed together as good friends do. Mary Kelly wanted to cheer up Joanna. She knew what a great catch Joanna was and how she adored kids.

"I thought he was nice," Joanna said. "Too bad he lives so far away, long distance you know...."

"There's always another guy," Mary Kelly said.

"Another fun date. Yeah!" Joanna said sarcastically flat, and they laughed. "Hey, I'm in for Brad for the long run."

"And girl it will be a long run. You may never reach the blue ribbon." Mary Kelly said.

"Oh he'll come around he's just moody," Joanna said.

The Passing of Summer

*J*oanna worked three days this week and each 12-hour stretch didn't seem to bother her the least. She was well rested from the last few weekends of fun. Having spent her time not only with Brad but also with a girlfriend, a group of people and a new guy, Joanna believed she was not dependent on Brad.

As she went out for a walk about the neighborhood and wildlife areas with Dancer, her dog, this Saturday morning, Joanna thought about the passing days. She picked up her pace to a jog as she met the dirt road that went on for what seemed like an eternity. By the post and rail fence, she stopped and unleashed Dancer giving a simple command with great excitement "Go". Dancer loved this game and took off running on an adventure in the desert wilderness. It was a game of seek and explore as there were rabbits, quail, lizards, shrubs, hills, rusty tin cans and old wood in various states of decay.

As Dancer chased animals and found new things to sniff, Joanna thought of Andy in California and about his active career as he went to sporting events and photo shoots. She jogged and walked and Dancer chased rabbits while Joanna took in the view. She never tired of the endless sky, the unpopulated desert and the saguaro cactus that stood so tall, like silent sentinels, they seemed to guard the undeveloped land. It was here she felt at peace.

At home, she poured a coffee and began to go through her stack of mail from the week. She opened a card and it was from Alex and Shawna announcing their marriage. It had been a family affair in Italy and a picture was enclosed. Joanna daydreamed about Italy, the music, the vineyards, and dancing with family relatives. It would've been like a movie. She was happy, happy for Alex as he was a great guy and a good friend in college.

Two weeks passed and there were no calls from Brad. Joanna was working on detaching her feelings. After almost a year of romance, Brad was still not ready for a serious relationship, and she figured spending less time together would help him realize how much he missed her. Then, the next Sunday afternoon he called to tell her everything that was happening at the hanger. The historical society was going to use his work and so on. It would be published this fall. He was so excited he wanted to see her himself to talk more about it. "Jo let me just take you for a ride in the convertible it's going to be a nice cool evening." He would pick her up.

She was out in front of her house in the front yard at six dressed in white crop pants and a green flowered button-up top from Ann Taylor, paired with her Louis Vuitton purse and sandals ... even in casual dress, Joanna was a natural beauty. Her hair was loose and curly falling way past her shoulders. As he arrived she looked up from the agave plant she was fussing with. "Joanna" he called.

She spun about to face him, "Hi there."

"Hey Jo," he said replacing his aviator style sunglasses on his face. He had jumped out of the car and was now by her side. He kissed her lightly on the lips. He was feeling so proud of himself. He opened the car door for her as he always did. In the car, he talked about the article and then stopped for a moment to complement Joanna on how pretty she looked. He had arrived in his 1999 Mercedes SLK 280 and they drove with the top open.

They went for ahi tuna fajitas at Oaxaca. At the restaurant, he spilled out the details and his excitement over the publication. "We are finally going to be getting recognition by documenting the connection of our plane to the Enola Gay as one of the original 15 B-29s. She was on in the same fleet...." Brad was so excited he talked about the project the entire dinner. Joanna just liked to hear his voice so when he was beyond her in the technical details she was still interested and would nod and look at him with wide eyes. On the way back they drove up the road by the walking path and stopped to sit on the big rock that bordered the park perimeter. They sat awhile chatting and then kissed as Brad declared his love for Joanna.

At Joanna's, they made love that night in the moonlight that came shining in across the room from the top of the wood blinds that covered the large windows. Her flowered sheets shimmering, the ruffled pillow shams stuffed with soft down and the French provincial furniture all added romance to the room.

Brad had laid her across the bed to unbutton her top and she made some silly remark laughing playfully. It was difficult for her to resist his affection. He smiled and kissed her neck, her shoulders, her middle, and slowly moved on down to the edge of her waistband. She welcomed his touch and his moist kisses. Encircling his neck and shoulders with her arms she moved her hips closer to him. He reached down and unbuttoned her crop pants button by button and slowly ran his hand down her legs as he slipped them off her. She sighed as her legs tingled with electricity when they rubbed against his bare hands and chest and she reached up to unzip his trousers. Stroking his firm thighs and abdomen the pleasure was hers. She kissed him on up to his chest and he held her closer to him cradling her. He nuzzled about her shoulders kissing her neck and together and away from their passion became rhythmic and heightened in one moment of pleasure.

As the moon rose and fell they slumbered awakening once again to make love. Later when the sun sparked the first light of the morning, he rose early for work, kissing her while she cooed. Again they made love and then slumbered for just a bit before Brad rose to dress. When he was leaving she got up to walk him out before returning to her bed and sinking into its soft moist sheets and the memory of their lovemaking.

Wednesday night Brad called just to chat and say how nice the time was that they had spent together. They made plans to go out on the weekend with another couple. The couple was a guy from Brad's office and his girlfriend. Saturday they got together and went to a movie about a woman and a man who lived by the ocean. She was an artist and he a ship builder and designer. The woman fell ill and the husband was left with his memories and her artwork with which he could not part. It was exciting but sad.

Later, Brad and Jo sat on her couch talking and watching late night TV. She was happy around him and she cuddled him as they sat on the couch. But Brad had more to say. Just holding hands and kissing he thought was leading her on and he said so. It's not like she was expecting a marriage proposal tonight, Joanna thought. She liked his friendship and admired his dedication to work and what seemed to her to be his honest lifestyle.

Soon she was feeling indifferent. His approach was confusing to Joanna. Did he not appreciate who she was, her intelligence, her company and the support she offered him? His see-saw attitude could be trying at times and just downright annoying and confusing to her. Finally, she said let's just not see each other anymore. They agreed as friends who care about each other's well-being. Then, in the next sentence, they made plans to call each other. He to see how her job went next week as she was the primary care nurse to a new infant & she to see how his latest car restoration was coming along. Brad was having an older jaguar restored, one his uncle and he had picked out at an auction.

So summer passed with sunny lazy days spent at the patio swimming in the pool with Dancer chasing her ball and neighbor friends like Sara and Mary Kelly coming to visit. Evenings when she wasn't working, there were calls and dates with Brad, a few group dates with some nurses and residents, or just a simple dinner alone with the TV.

The last weekend in August was the ASU Alumni Lake party. Her alumni met at the marina for a fish fry and boating. Saguaro Lake was South of Troon Mt and a nice drive thru town and out again into the desert by the river. She parked in the gravel lot. On the upper balcony of the marina, colorfully dressed in shorts and swimsuit outfits and hats and sandals were about 30 alumni. Saying her hellos Joanna walked table to table and found a spot where some younger people sat, everyone at different stages of the meal. "The fish is great." Joanna sat with some guys and girls she knew, Tara, Michael, and Susan.

Hi, Joanna." Alex said as he walked up. "Is this seat available?"

Alex was her hiking friend from geology. They had hiked the Grand Canyon with the group and hung out occasionally as classmates. "Hey, yourself!"

"How's my other girl?"

Joanna laughed, "great my love." Alex and his girlfriend, now wife, had been together for years, yet Joanna and Alex had their own flirtation. "How's the rock pile?" Joanna said meaning Alex's career in land development and they bust out laughing. Joanna always did have a way of bringing out his humorous side. They had always got on well bumping into each other at events and such being in the same college departments. Alex and Shawna were now married, their wedding was this past Spring. Shawna was out with her sisters today for some special party. Brad was visiting his uncle in San Francisco for a car auction. Joanna never let his absence stop her from going out to parties and events. Alex talked briefly about his newest development in the valley.

Alex reminded Jo of Brad, not just their physique but their manner was similar. They were both diligent in their work dedicated and serious yet kind. Both were adventurous and social at parties and both enjoyed the out of doors. She liked his attention and talking with him. Joanna and Alex relived the Grand Canyon Hike and the overnight at Phantom Ranch. "Remember how we hid behind the rocks and scarred Mike into running back to the bunk house," Alex remarked. They laughed.

"My favorite was swimming under the waterfalls," said Joanna. "... the energy of the falling water, the green plants hanging over the ledges with those tiny purple flowers. It was all sooo beautiful and magical."

"I remember seeing the layers of Coconino sandstone for the first time..," Alex paused and changed his thought. "That and you in the water with that tiny thing you gals call a suit."

"Oh stop," Joanna laughed

"Hey, guys." It was Carol. "Is this the most beautiful night? It's cool enough to venture outdoors if you're near water."

"Oh but it's a dry heat," they mocked, as Carol's husband Jim wiped his brow.

The group talked through dinner, as people came and went table to table. And as the dinner finished, Susan and Joanna strolled out to the lawn and down the steps tot the docks. Susan was a bit loud and almost rude at times which is all that prevented the two women from being the best of friends. Susan was selling real estate a big leap from zoology class. Eventually, they all gathered out front by the boats.

On the dock, all four captains were hollering come on board. Joanna strategically jumped into the boat. To her surprise, Alex jumped in after her. The water was deep blue as was the sky even with its half moon and the mountains rose from all sides of the lake. It was truly a beautiful site. Joanna, Susan, Carol, Jim, Michael, Ben, and Alex spent a good time at the bow of the boat sipping wine and sodas, telling stories, and enjoying good old friendships as the wake and water spray misted the evening air. Jim and Dan were at the stern steering. All the boats having circled the lake later arrived at the wooden docks from which they had departed. Hugs and goodbyes followed, and then people walked toward their cars.

"We should get together sometime," Alex said as he walked Jo to her car. Joanna smiled. "The four of us could go to the Pinnacle for drinks and dinner or something."

"Yes, that would be great," Joanna replied but she knew this wouldn't work. Shawna would be snooty and bored and Brad would be reserved yet polite and the only two having real great conversation would be Alex and Jo

It had been a fun day the kind you see in movies and TV. It was a great end of summer and welcome to fall. The dark and coolness of the night air was welcoming. Stars were twinkling in the distance. Joanna got in her car and drove home singing to the radio "...*Ba..ay...be, You're my a...a...angel come and make it alright. Come and save tonight. Your the reason I live, your the reason I die, there be no reason why. Ba... ay... be my a... ngel come and save me tonight....*"

September 13 was a Friday. Joanna waded in her pool tossing Dancer's ball, she hoped Sara would call and invite her over. Out in the side yard, she checked on Mikie and Yoddle her desert tortoises. Putting out a handful of lettuce and spinach, she spied Mikie. "Come here boy." She picked him up and peered into his face as his neck stretched out to bob his head up and down. "Mikie! Does Mikie like it? You just tell Yoddle to come out of her hole this is your favorite season." Around in the back, she dropped into the chair holding Mikie. Even with her house full of pets it seemed too quiet at home today. She didn't know what to do with herself. She wandered back in the house. She busied herself with fixing and putting away clothes and things.

Sara called at 10:00. "Sue is here and I called Mindy too. Come on over if you want to we're going to make lunch. But just to warn you there's a lot of kids here." Joanna accepted with exclamation she only wished she had a daughter to bring over too. She cared for babies at work and pets at home but that couldn't match a daughter. She gathered her things and some oatmeal cookies. At the door, she also placed a small cooler with some homemade lemonade, as she turned from the refrigerator and all in a moment she realized the date. The calendar on the wall seemed to jump out at her. What used to mark the welcome change of seasons and the start of the fall semester the month of September had a different meaning for Joanna. The song that played in her head was there again. "It was the third of September... a day I'll always remember." It was about a mother telling her child that his father was gone. Four years ago today was the day that changed her life forever, the car accident that happened long ago.

She wandered into her house away from the kitchen. Standing by her front door she looked down at her collection of photographs of people whom she loved. Each frame was special and each photo marked an event. She picked up one of the framed photos and stared at it for several minutes and out loud she said, "Mom, dad I love you, I wish you were here.... I would make you dinner in my nice house." She recalled the many home cooked dinners her mother made for her and the after dinner evenings spent on her parent's porch. Sometimes there were just the three of them and sometimes joining them were her parent's friends or Joanna's classmates.

Joanna and her mom would cut vegetables and make salads and fruit pies in the kitchen while talking about everything from her studies to boyfriends and world news. Their kitchen was light green with light green and white checked drapes over the windows and plants on the sill. Sometimes there were several ladies in the kitchen, including Joanna's roommate or her mom's friend Lacey. Never was there an aunt as Celeste was an only child like Joanna. Joanna's dad had no sisters only brothers and his family was back in Boston. Joanna would drink mineral water and her mom drank coffee as they worked over the kitchen counters chatting and laughing while adding spices and tasting the homemade dishes. Her dad would peer in now and then, being charming and flirtatious. His office had a Lionel train that ran around its perimeter high on the wall. He collected the small train cars over his lifetime since childhood. He was also a reader of books and a watcher of TV. When Joanna was a child he would read to her prose and stories and such.

She paused with a long silence in her thoughts. She wandered back to her kitchen. Leaning back into the counter still holding the frame, she quietly said, "At least you are together. I'm all by myself. Why daddy? Why?" A tear appeared at the corner of her eye and then began to run down her cheek. She made no attempt to catch it. Her breath became shallow and short. Her chest heaved as she traced their figures in the photo and fought the tears. She longed to touch them for real. She longed to hug her mother and to say how much she appreciated the time in the kitchen, the long talks, and the baking lessons. She longed to apologize for things she had done wrong. She longed to be read to by her father just one more time or to read with him in his office as they had done when she was doing research in college. If only she could thank him for being there, for being her dad, for loving her, and in his own way taking care of her family.

Together their life had seemed peaceful and complete. Joanna cried out loud, a cry from deep within her soul, and then she sobbed. With her hands on her face, she pushed away the tears and gasped for air. "Daddy," she cried as if she could call him back. "Daa...ddy," she called. No one would answer. Looking at the photo her chest was heaving, she recalled that as old as they were, her parents had still held hands and some days they kissed in front of Joanna. The last day she had seen them was out in front of their house. They had turned around to walk back into their house pausing to wave goodbye from the front porch railing. They stood together, her mother and dad, holding hands, he in his khaki trousers and her mother in a summer skirt.

Joanna's tone changed from warm to wanting. "You're missing it," Joanna exclaimed, "everything, my house, my career, Brad, Sara". She sunk to the floor feeling her deep sorrow as if it had never been released from her soul. "How could you leave me?" She sat there just staring. Moments passed and Joanna took a breath and moved to the present. While still sitting on the floor she spoke to them .... "I save little tiny babies, families about to begin. They are little miracles." She was living a full life now she reminded herself as she stood up. And she promised as she always did in her quiet talks like this that she would be out and about and meet people as often as she could, and she would go on and be successful and they could be proud of the beginning they gave her. They would be proud of her strength and how she was outgoing and friendly like her mother and smart and loving like her father.

"Someday I will have a family too. Sara is married with a wonderful family." She said to the photo frame. And with that thought, she was again wistful. "Everyone here is married. Married, married why in my face always their children their house their family parties." She recalled Janie's birthday passed and she had not been invited. "Oh Joanna," Sara said, "it was just the family you know, family and wild kids." Joanna wanted to be Janie's aunt in pretend. She was, after all, Sara's best friend. But Sara had sisters and sisters-in-law and while all Sara ever wanted was a little time alone, Joanna hoped for more time with her and her family. Truly in this way, the two women were like opposites.

Joanna put the picture of her parents and herself, which was framed in the deep cherry wood back on the hall table. She sighed and took a deep breath. "I promise," she said quietly. Reaching down she picked up her beach bag went to the sink and splashed water on her face. She wiped her beach towel across her eyes and cheeks, opened the door and off she went to Sara's a short walk down the street.

The ladies sunned themselves on reclining pool chairs and drank lemonade in Sara's backyard. Occasionally they dipped in the pool or lay on blown up silver rafts. They ran after the children with sunscreen and colored beach towels and Popsicles. They dodged balls and such all while talking gardening and men and children.

Late that afternoon, Joanna went to see her mom and dad as she did each September. She drove to the countryside outside Tempe where the buildings were few and the sky seemed clear of clutter.

She brought daisies and an ornamental metal and glass garden figurine, which in its abstract nature seem to belong on a psychologist's desk. In the glow of the sun not yet set, she walked alone down the path to the spot she knew well, to be with what was hers and hers alone, her mom and dad. She sunk into the earth at their carved headstone. With her fingers and palms, she caressed their headstone. She prayed for their happiness, their togetherness and said words of love. Quietly she sat portraying acceptance and feeling her present truth of gratitude for the loving past from which she had come.

Joanna patted the ground. "Mommy? " Joanna choked. "Mommy I brought you flowers." Tears came into and filled her eyes. "They are daisies." She stopped herself and then became very quiet as she immersed herself in a vision of the past. Looking up at her mom while holding her hand, Joanna was a child once again at the zoo. "Tigers have to stay in the zoo." Her mom said. Then she was holding a turtle, a big turtle, and her mom snapped a photo with the old Kodak camera. Then years later she was leaving their house, "bye, bye dear," her mother said. "The sweater is lovely dear." (It was a gift Joanna had given her for their trip to Europe).

"Have a great time," Joanna called back from her car. Her mom and dad stood waving on the porch her mom with the sweater over her arm, her dad in his plaid shirt and khaki pants, "Drive careful now." her father said as he always did.

"Mom? Daddy?" Joanna asked as if to hear an answer. "Daddy I thought you would like this." She arranged the figurine with the daisies. "Remember how we used to listen to music and dance to the Beatles? Remember Crosby Stills how you played that song on your guitar? It was *Guinevere... had green eyes like yours...* the song played in the background of her thoughts. I wanted you to be at my wedding and walk with me. I thought we would dance a Beatles song. She smiled. She was quiet and then she implored, "I wanted you to dance with me, daddy. Why did you leave me? I miss you. I... I... need a family too." Again, little tears appeared at corners of her eyes again and began to roll down her cheeks. "I want to be married, daddy. Oh, mom, you're the one I could talk to. If only we could have been making potato salad today, with the little peas from the garden. I'd give anything to...be with you today..." Her words had trailed off and out loud she was crying. And in that moment, she became more like the little girl that was lost inside her. Outward a grown woman is what everyone saw but inside this part of her that no one saw still lived. Joanna wiped her cheeks. She had promised herself not to cry this time. This time, she would give only thanks she had told herself. She gazed up at the sky while leaning on her side, stroking the grassy lawn about her.

Joanna's parents had been on a trip to Europe. Joanna had gotten the call one Tuesday morning from her mother's best friend. "Are you home dear? I'm coming right over."

"Oh, Lacey I'm just about to go to class. I have students. This is the beginning of the year! My students are...."

"Please wait, now I've something to tell you right away." She came over to Joanna's apartment immediately.

Joanna invited her into the little campus apartment. "Your father and mother had a car accident and your mother has suffered a brain hemorrhage."

"No!" Joanna screamed. "No." Through her tears, all she could say is "No... no". Then, "Are you sure? It's not her, it can't be!" Joanna stood in the front room of her condo with Lacey looking so helpless as she could not say the worst that she had to say. How could she tell her that her only family was....

In her thoughts, she struggled to coach herself. 'Just the basics,' Lacey reminded herself...just as she had told herself on the drive over, 'just a bit at a time'.

Joanna looking at Lacey implored her, "That is really bad Lacey, isn't it? That's bad," she said as she clutched the woman's arms and drew her nearer. Looking at her face searching for details Joanna sniffled. "She's not going to die...is she going to? Oh mom, mom, will she ever be the same? What are they doing? I have to go to her."

"Of course, you do and I'm here to make your flight and help you, Joanna. I love you like my own daughter now whatever I can do."

"I have to ...umm... to pack," Joanna said as she ran across her apartment and disappeared into her bedroom still in shock. Then moments later she reappeared demanding Lacey reassure her. "Will she be OK?" Joanna cried. "Lacey let's call the hospital." Joanna sniffled. "I have to talk to my father. I need to talk to daddy. Oh, daddy what will we do if mom ... if she ...dies?" Joanna dropped to the floor by her counter and cried.

Lacey put her arm around Joanna's shoulder. "Your flight deal, that is first, we will get through this. I wish I could go with you. Who can go with you?" Lacey said.

"I have to call daddy how did he sound?"

"It's difficult Joanna, I know. Now be a tough girl and let's make your plans," Lacey responded.

Joanna breathed in "OK. I'm OK now. The class just started Lacey, everyone has class, there's orientation and who will cover my labs and classes ... and maybe Anna. Anna will go with me. My passport!" Joanna trailed off into her bedroom again. She threw clothes on her bed and began looking for her passport. Lacey followed her.

"How do we call Anna?" Lacey got the information out of Joanna and went from the bedroom to the living room once again. She called the University to get a hold of Anna. Then using Joanna's computer she tried to connect with airlines. Soon she gave up and dialed the airlines. "Yes, a low-cost fare but right away. Bereavement fare? Yes, oh that's nice. I ah, OK tomorrow I've got it, J OA N N A STYLES, ANNA... KEMPER," she spelled out.

Joanna reappeared in the kitchen. "Lacey the airfare, I can use my charge card but Anna can I... can ah, it's got to be over a thousand dollars. She just started her assistant professorship."

"Dear I have it, let me pay for it. We'll balance things out later."

"Oh, Lacey what would I do without you?" Joanna wined.

"You would do fine," Lacey replied preparing her for what was to come. "You have the strength of your mother. You have been so strong, so independent."

"Daddy... Lacey, how is daddy? Let's talk to him, try to get him, Lacey. What's the hospital name what's number, who called you?" Joanna said as she picked up her phone and held it as she walked toward the living room couch about to sit down. "I have to...."

"Joanna," Lacey said quietly now interrupting her, "your dad was hurt too."

"Daddy? Oh, daddy how is he I thought it was mom." Lacey walked across the living room toward Joanna. The distance across the tiny kitchen seemed like an eternity to Joanna. The woman Joanna knew as Lacey, who was wearing a beige dress and sandals, blended into the beige walls of Joanna's apartment. Everything became wavy and so far away. Time and space blended together for Joanna and for a moment the world seemed fuzzy like a dream like a really, really bad dream. Lacey seemed to move in slow motion as she walked toward her.

Joanna had sunk to the floor just in front of the couch. Lacey picked her up and sat her on the couch. She looked straight into Joanna's eyes as softly as she could but very seriously and she said, "Now listen we don't know exactly Joanna but it's very serious and they are both in intensive care. You need to trust that the doctors are doing everything they can. It's best you just go to them as soon as you can." Joanna felt as if she could never breathe again. Lacey sat down next to Joanna and put an arm around her shoulders to comfort her.

"It's those stupid drivers I heard all about their highways over there. Some idiot just probably raced them off the road."

"This is all that we know and all you can do is pray and go to them. Honey, you have all had a good life they are together, they are in good hands."

"In Spain?" Joanna exclaimed through her tears almost in a mocking laugh and now getting angry.

"How can they be in good hands when they're not even in their own country?"

Her roommate Anna had insisted on going with her. The two young women were student professors and assistant professors in different departments. Their students would be taught by other assistants. It was after all the beginning of the academic year so the University and the students would be OK without them. Anna feared, however, that Joanna might never be OK.

That next day they were flying to Spain. When they arrived Anna took Joanna to the hospital and the ICU. Her father and her mom shared a room. "Senorita venaca con mi lo siento mi child." (Come with me, my poor child). The nurse greeted her with sentiments of sympathy and walked her to a room. "Aque esta tu mamma y tu padre. You see them, you talk it's OK." Her father had passed before she arrived. Across the room by the window, he lay in his bed. He was so still so quiet as if he was sleeping. He looked just like daddy sleeping on the couch except very pale and the covers were tucked in around him so neatly. His lips were pale and chapped. His life support had been removed just prior to Joanna's visit. From the last airport phone, she had given them permission to turn off the ventilator and remove his life support. The staff had done their best to make him look like he was resting. The covers were folded just below his chin across his shoulders. His chest had been crushed by the steering wheel and his heart was extensively damaged.

"We are trying to keep his heart going and lungs working for you to see him." The voice of the doctor on the phone had said early in the morning. It had been almost two days since the accident with the flight time and all.

"And I can still see him without the equipment? You will keep him with mom I will be there shortly? Are you sure? He would not want to be kept on machines.... I have to hold him, to see him with mommy one more time." Joanna cried. "He's my dad."

The nurse held the door while Joanna and the doctor walked into the room. She was now as strong as she could be and the sight before her was something the staff had tried to prepare her for. She kissed her mom before going to her father in the next bed. She took his hand, "It's OK daddy it's OK I'll take care of mommy and you rest, you rest now daddy." She stroked his head and patted his chest as tears ran down her cheeks. She was half in the bed with him reaching her arms out. Gently she patted his chest, "I love you, I always will." She kissed him. His face was cool and speckled with cuts. She wanted to crawl up next to him and hold him, to sit in his lap one more time. There were many pictures running thru her mind and tears clouding her eyes before rolling down her cheeks." Daddy," she said. "It's OK daddy, I'm here, I'm right here," she said. Then she asked as if he was listening, "I have to talk to mom OK?" She spoke as if her father could hear as if he was listening. I'll be back. I love you." She stretched out her one arm and then led herself across the room with her other arm.

She almost tip-toed to her mother's bedside. "Mom it's me, Joanna. Mom, I love you I'm here now everyone is taking good care of you. They say you are the best patient." And that made Joanna cry again. Of course, she was a good patient, she couldn't move. "Mom they did surgery and you will be a while but I know you'll be fine soon." She looked at her mom, her eyes closed, a bandage on her head, and from her mouth was a plastic tube that connected to a machine that breathed for her. Her skin was pink and warm as Joanna rested her hand on her mother's thigh, afraid to touch anything else. Always Celeste had been such a strong woman always talking and social and now she was quiet

That's all Joanna remembered, that, and the day they turned off her mother's ventilator. "OK, now it's OK." She had said. "We're ready huh mommy?" It was a moment in time where no one could reach her. She heard only her own breath and a hum of the Spanish language in the background. She sobbed over her mom, and Anna, who had been holding Joanna's hand, slipped out of the room taking the nurses with her.

Joanna lay across her mother as if to hold on to life itself. Her legs were dangling off the bed while her arms were wrapped over her mom. She held tight to the blankets on the other side of the bed as she draped herself over her mother. Joanna turned her own head to the side peering up at her mom's face. The woman who had loved Joanna so dearly was leaving this world forever. The white walls of the room surrounded them. Then there was a flash of light. Light so bright it was as if in a dream. It startled Joanna. It was a dream she had later told herself. Everything went white and there were her mom and dad, together, side by side, standing tall and high up looking down on her so pleasant looking and softly saying "love you, dear, always we do love you and we will be right here." The next thing she recalled was boarding the flight for home.

Her parent's bodies would make the same trip.

As the plane lifted, one by one buildings and fountains became tiny. Spires from churches, flags from high poles, and castle towers all disappeared one by one. She was now merely a woman on a plane.

She picked up her iPod without setting it to any song. She placed the earphones over her ears and it was in the middle of a Sara McLaughlin song. When she heard the singing, it was like an angel singing to her... like a message meant just for her... "*and life's too long ... long and cold... here without you... I grieve in my condition cause I cannot find the words to say I need you so....*" The voice, the words, and music made Joanna feel connected as if her mom and dad were grieving her same grief of separation, as if it was a message from an angel, from them. "*and I for... got to tell ... you I love you....*" She sighed again giving in to the tears which soon filled her eyes. She made no sound as she was exhausted and she let her head fall back against the headrest, replacing her sunglasses over her eyes. The tears went on and trickled behind her glasses and down her face as she surrendered to the music. Anna leaned over and put her arm around Joanna and said nothing, offering her all that one who is grieving ever wants, quiet presence.

Now sitting on the ground at their family plot in Tempe sat Joanna. A plane flew overhead and brought Joanna back to the present. The sun was setting. She took a tissue from her pocket and wiped her cheeks. "Oh," Joanna sighed, "Brad, ah, I almost forgot about Brad." She took a breath into the present. "I wish you could meet him. He's so nice. Mom, he works hard and he never misses a day ....", she trailed off. "He flies planes and he collects cars. Daddy, you would like that, you two with your trains and cars. He's taking me to dinner." Slowly she stood up, "I have to go now." Her last words, as she stood up, were the same ones she said each year. "I love you always." With those words said, she turned and walked away from the gravesite. Just above the ornate headstone, a white cloud of light shimmered, and Joanna's silhouette, outlined by the blue sky, became smaller and smaller as she walked to her car.

As Joanna drove home the song that came on the radio was *'Dance with my Father Again'*. She began to hum the tune and instead of being sad, she thought lovingly of how it would be as she pictured herself with her dad dancing. And rather than a tear, a slow smile came across her lips as she fondly remembered him.

That night, Brad came by with takeout dinner. He called to say he was on his way over. and how about Chinese. Afterward, they sat on the patio enveloped by the deep blue night sky. The two had squeezed into one lounge chair and lay in each other's arms. They sat and gazed at the stars. The blue sky reflected in the pool. In the distance now and then a coyote howled. It had been a long day. Joanna felt safe and loved here with Brad. He picked out stars and told her the story of Orion again. Joanna was soothed just by the sound of his voice in the night air. He knew that she had been to the cemetery, he didn't have to ask. She wouldn't say much about it. Brad called his family about every other Sunday almost without fail. He knew if his mom died he would dearly miss her.

Later they went inside and slept thru the night. In the morning, they ate breakfast, walked Dancer and swam about the pool. Then Brad went home to take care of things. He'd wash his car, sort mail and pick up odd things at the stores as his usual Saturday. He called her later in the day but made no plans.

"What are you doing Brad?" Joann replied.

"Nothing really just tired you know it was a long week. These projections have been keeping me late at the office. You can come over if you want or maybe tomorrow we'll do something I'm just going to mellow out here a while, maybe watch the game...." his words trailed off. She wasn't really listening now.

If ever there was a man who could live alone it was Brad. He could just hang out, go to the gym or watch TV. He was a simple man nothing flamboyant about him. He wasn't sports crazy or girl crazy. When there was some big project at work and so he would go in at 7 and work at a desk until 6:30 every day. Jo wondered how he could do that every day she looked forward to her days off. What would life be without time to walk on the land to sit by the pool to talk with the girls or sleep in now and then? He never slept in, even at her house when he stayed it was a challenge to stay in bed. I guess he made up for his long weeks all on the weekend hence his alone time, his TV and laundry day, and shopping day. He cooked simply and liked to iron his own shirts. Not that Jo was spoiled, while her friends had housekeepers, lawn people and other people to repair things Jo did most everything herself only having an occasional lawn and tree service and Brad to help her.

"What about tomorrow? Brad said.

"That's OK, tomorrow is fine." Sometimes she was irritated by his kick back lack of action and adventure attitude and sometimes it seemed just right. Today, she was hoping to have company. She hung out with Dancer painted some wooden bird-cages she had picked up at the hobby shop and listened to the radio on her patio. She called Mary Kelly to tell her of her artsy day and Mary Kelly insisted that Joanna come over later to have a glass of wine and to show off her artwork.

At Mary Kelly's, the two women sat in the living room sipping wine while Manny took the kids out for ice cream. "This is a nice break for me," Mary Kelly said. "Sometimes when he's gone, on the road selling artwork and setting up shows, I have them all week, day and night by myself. But when he's here, he's a great dad. I have to keep on him about the house, though. You'd think he could notice that things need fixing. Just because I paint doesn't mean I'm the handy one. I don't know what to do," she exclaimed. "I called his brother Tuesday because the garage door broke. I couldn't get the car out. I had to walk the baby to school to pick up Ellie and it's 100 degrees out. Then the repairman, who knows if he's telling me that I need extras just because I have no clue about mechanics."

"I know exactly what you mean Mary K, I always have to call Brad or someone for advice."

"How's things with you two Jo? Is he getting over that friend's thing he has? I swear if Manny had said he was just friends I'd be long gone." She paused. "But then a friendship makes for a solid foundation."

"He doesn't say 'just friends' he just emphasizes it like what we have comes around every day."

"It doesn't Jo and maybe he needs to realize that, and so do you. Don't you spend forever waiting especially if you want to have kids? I mean you've got to want your own family." Joanna suddenly looked sullen. "I'm sorry," Mary Kelly said.

"It's OK it happens every September."

"What?" Joann made no reply. "Oh, This is when it happened huh?" Joanna nodded as her face flushed. "Well, you got us, Jo." Mary Kelly put an arm around her before getting up to go to the kitchen. "Come on, I want to show you something." She said wanting to brighten their mood.

In the kitchen, she refilled their wine glasses with the crisp Russian River Valley chardonnay from California. Off the kitchen, was a door to her studio. The two women stepped inside. "I just ordered these," Mary Kelly said standing at her desk. "It's metallic paint. This has real pieces of bronze and copper in it! And... in the silver, there's like flecks but all different sizes so it hits the light and changes."

"Wow, that would look great on my bird house."

"I'm going to use them in abstract landscapes I think. Why don't you come over and paint with me one day this coming week."

"It would be fun."

"Yeah, and you can try some metallic paint."

They were smiling as they returned to the living room sipping wine from the crystal glasses. Mary Kelly got out some rich dark chocolate from a client-patron in Belgium. The chocolate was so fresh that the heavenly aroma filled their senses even before each piece was all unwrapped. As the night progressed the two women sunk into the comfort of the vanilla brocade couch in Mary Kelly's living room and talked for hours into the night. It was late when Joanna went home.

On Sunday Brad called. He talked about John at work and Mark his Jr. accountant. John was always in the forefront of things, being known, having things to say. That was what Joanna heard, and the Jr. accountants like Mark were less serious about work than Brad thought they should be. Joanna felt she could write a book about his associates at the office with all the info he gave her on them. She was happy though that he enjoyed what he did and he seemed to take great pride in his accomplishments. Recently he had been working on some plans for their L.A. office.

After a long chat, they decided to go to the mall because Brad wanted to look at dress shirts. It was a warm day as usual in the desert so the mall probably was a good place to be. Brad found his shirts at Nordstrom. They all were blue or blue striped. Joanna bought a shirt too, a casual top with flowers and tassels and some other details by Peace Universe. So this was their Sunday and after shopping, they had a sandwich at a nearby restaurant.

Later at Joann's house, Brad stepped in after they parked his car. In the hallway, they kissed good-bye. "I missed you, Jo. It's been a long few days."

"I missed you too," Brad replied by gazing at her, his eyes sparkling. She kissed him back with more passion. He leaned into her accepting her advance and returning her kisses. While caressing her neck he pressed his lips to hers and then kissed her on down her cheek to her chest. His fingers entangled in her long locks and she leaned back to enjoy his touch. His arms held her tight while their hips pressed together. Joanna twirled around and tugged at his arm toward the hallway that led to the bedroom. He smiled and they laughed. She pulled her shirt over her head and dropped it on the floor. He was now feeling her breasts covered in a black lace bra. She unbuttoned his shirt in the hall and stroked his chest, leaning into him. "Here?" he said.

She smiled coyly and moved her hands to his waist. As he stepped out of his trousers, he bent over to slide his hands down Joanna's unbuttoned jeans feeling her toned shapely legs as the denim fell to the floor. "They don't call these jeans Lucky Jeans for nothing," Jo said, and they both laughed as he pressed her against the wall kissing her breasts as she guided him close to her.

"Oh, Babe ...."

"Brad," she called for him. "Umm." They sighed as they joined in the pleasure that unites love. They breathed deep and stared wide eye at one another. He lifted her legs and carried her around the corner to the bedroom and to the bed where they lay next to one another for a while just peacefully dozing in their dampness. They awoke and soon they were again tangled up as lovers touching kissing hungry for the love they made and shared. Brad bathed in her beauty and the feel of her skin next to his, sighing and breathing hard. He was as firm as she was smooth. Joanna welcomed his affection and moved with him. They lay quiet. Then Jo jumped up. "I need to wear these jeans more often." She said as she went to get Dancer from the patio and some soda from the kitchen.

Together they lounged on her bed watching a movie. When the movie ended Brad kissed her goodbye. "I'll call you later Jo," he said and she and Dancer watched as he got back in his Mercedes and drove off. It was that kind of familiarity that was comfortable about the relationship. Neither one of them always had to be on. Joanna went to her bed feeling content as she sunk into her sheets.

Fall was the busy time at the NICU with many births and the holidays. Joanna had no problem getting extra shifts. She worked three days and sometimes four and then sometimes two just for a rest. As challenging was her job it was also tiring. Some days she missed lunch and stayed late, as did everyone. Everything seemed so urgent.

One day on the way home she stopped at the grocery and the check our lady, Shirley, said to her as she walked thru in her scrubs, "Do you like it, working in the hospital?"

Out of Joanna's mouth came, "Oh my I feel like a construction worker." She had no time to eat anything that day except a cookie, her hair was messed, her scrubs spotted and wrinkled, and her eyes were darkened by smudged mascara, but more obvious to her weariness was her posture. She leaned her head to one side, her arms rested heavily on the grocery counter and her body seemed to sit back on her hips. At this moment, she was appreciating that she wore sneakers for work and there were only a few more steps to home.

Later that week, talking to Sara she said, "you know if I make a mistake it could be fatal. It's not like someone goes home with the wrong bag of groceries. A few weeks ago a nurse had placed the lipids on the feeding line and the feeding on the lipid line. They both came in 30 cc syringes from the pharmacy both kept cold in the refrigerator and both were identically a milky white. The big difference, however, is that the lipids were specially made to run in the venous line directly into the bloodstream while the formula is a food substance only for the stomach and they were labeled so.

Soon after the hanging of the syringes, the infant became ill. His sats (oxygen saturation reading) dropped, his heart rate failed, everyone did everything and it was another day before he died and then they found that this was the error that killed this baby. Cathy, the nurse was a wreck already, as would be anyone with the loss of life yet an infant in her charge, to be the one that made the error, an error that ended the baby's life."

"I don't know how you do it Jo, I have enough commotion right here at home."

"That nurse was a divorced mother with three children. She was suspended and later terminated."

"After that," Joann continued, "all the lipid syringes were made with new Leur lock adapters that were incompatible with the tubing that went to the feeding lines and so this error could not be duplicated even if someone was busy or so hurried and so they failed to double check."

But Joanna, she was a checker always double-checking. In her earlier days of nursing, she was once reprimanded by a boss on the medical-surgical unit who told her to stop checking. She replied with the power that was her choice to assume stating, "ah, but this is our system of checks and balances, much like what our government has. It is my job, my duty and ...my butt!" Her tone was pleasant yet firm. Standing in front of her boss she opened the patient chart and compared the pharmacy label on the IV bag with the doctor's orders.

"Have you no trust?" her boss quipped.

"Checks and balances," she repeated as she initialed the bag, "My butt." And she ran off.

With fall also came school sports for Sara's children and Mary Kelly's children. Some days Joanna went with Sara to Tracy and Lindsey's games. Joanna on the sideline cheered the goals and wooed the falls. Secretly she wished to be a soccer mom and have children running about the house like Sara and as much as Sara complained, Joanna knew she liked being a mom.

Sara was not the best sister substitute for Jo as much as Jo tried to be a sister to Sara, Sara had sisters of her own with children who were cousins to her children. Now with the activities that Sara was into - mother daughter brownies, homework, soccer mother meetings, and making dinner for the family Sara was very busy. She even quit her part-time job at the recreation center and became a homeroom mom. Sara's sisters came over on holidays and birthdays and it was easy for her family to visit her sister's house as she had children to entertain Janie, Tracy, and Lindsey. Joanna was very aware that she was still single and it began to seem like her true calling was to be something other than a mommy. When Joanna would mention her wish to have kids, her older friend at work would say, "You can have my kids."

Moms surrounded Joanna. There always a mom to remark about how wonderful their care was at the hospital. Also in the neighborhood a lady had moved in whose twins had been born at St. Mary's where Jo worked and although Jo wasn't the nurse to care for them she was aware of who they were. The mom, Ethel, was able to relate her experience and her concerns to Jo. Some days they had walked the neighborhood in the early morning. Yet this friendship did not last. Ethyl was very frightened of the desert creatures like snakes and scorpions and coyotes and so concerned at the possibility that mountain lions could appear in the wildlife areas surrounding the houses and possibly jump the fence that the family moved back down into the valley to an area on the west side called Glendale.

Although Joanna did not have her own children she was a mom in her own way. She would say at the clubs, " I have two or three children three days a week, and then I go home to peace and quiet!"

Toward the end of October Brad planned a special trip and he and Joanna flew to Sedona. The red rocks were always an amazing site to see. It was the anniversary of when they met and they planned a hike and day trip. It was a grand day. Brad had gone all out to rent the plane and afford the gas. In the back of the piper cub, he had crammed in their bikes. High in the sky, they saw Phoenix like a toy train track set with its suburban layout. Flying over mountains and desert land, as they got closer to Sedona the rocks became redder. Soon the landing strip was ahead. Brad circled the area for a second look. He lowered the plane and then whoosh, back up the nose went.

"Brad?"

"Let's try it again co-pilot ready?" He circled the plane around, climbed in altitude and then again descending and woosh up they went. "Just want to make sure Jo, the strip is narrow up here."

Again the plane lowered and Joanna was now concerned. She thought of George Kennedy and his wife Carolyn, their last trip together was in a small plane like this. They crashed somewhere in the ocean, didn't they? She had been planning on living a bit longer. She studied his face. Was he worried? The plane was falling fast.

"Hold on Joann!" The landing strip was coming at them or they at it. A bang brought out the landing gear and the banging continued against the ground. They were landing fast.

"Whew that was a steep one! I haven't done this in a while I guess. What a primitive strip, you'd think they'd get with the times." He was smiling all proud of himself and he eyed Joanna with excitement and yearning. She just looked at him for a moment or two before she broke a grin and they climbed out of the plane.

He unloaded their bikes and made arrangements with the guys at the hanger for the plane. Joanna road her 10-speed TREK. The black bike frame shimmered in the sun with its bright pink and lime green details. Brads YETI was silver blue. He bought it from Colorado store where an engineer designed specialty bikes. The ride on Airline Road was all downhill. As one would imagine they were on the top of a mountain peak. Just down around the red rock-lined road was the shopping area. Along the main street, they stopped and picked up drinks. They walked past several tourist stores where southwest jewelry and pottery was sold. On past the shops, they biked to the creek, removed their shoes and took a walk along the creek bed hopping over rocks and peering at ponds of fish and frogs.

While walking creek side, Brad commented to Joanna about moving along in the relationship. "Let's sit and talk Joanna there's something I want to say." Joanna and Brad found a huge flat rock, crawled up, and searching his face for more meaning, she let him talk. "We get along well and there comes time.... I know you want to, well we need to decide where we are going and I was thinking we could live together." His words surprised her, no shocked her. Jo searching his face for more meaning more words, let him talk. Brad continued. "I think of you all the time," he said as if to show his sincerity. Joanna just looked at him not sure which way to go with that. She was happy and sad all at once. "What's wrong Jo? Jo?"

She seemed to be pouting. She wanted the ring the wedding the family part of it all and to celebrate. It seemed to her that it would not work if he was going into it half-heartedly. "Live together Brad?" Jo said. "It's not like I'm 20!"

"Well I know, but my parents and my brother...." (she knew they had been divorced).

"I don't think I'd be proud," Brad. She paused thoughtfully. "I wouldn't want to call everyone and say I have great news we are living together."

"But we could spend more time together."

They sat on a rock. She loved Brad and wanted to be with him she had not dreamed of the day he would ask her to live with him. She thought, though, if they became engaged he could move in and they would have time to make wedding plans while they lived together.

"Jo I ... Jo I do like you a lot." And finally, he said very quietly "You know I love you," and he wrapped his arms around her and smiled a big smile. "Joooannnna." He gazed upon her as he was feeling so pleased with himself for making this declaration for being ready to move forward. Joanna responded with a smile returning his kisses as she always did when his arms were around her. The thought of not being with him was too painful and she felt so loved despite what she thought was his awkwardness with words about love and commitment. She knew that he had never had a long-term relationship even in college. He was always a student focused on work and success, while she had, during her college years, a few long- term relationships. She knew she was Brad's one and only love.

They walked with his arm around her for a bit, they hiked and looked at rocks and squirrels and waded in the creek. Then after a Mexican lunch at Javelina Cantina, they biked back up airline road!! "Awesome!" Jo exclaimed all breathy.

"Pure ascent!" Brad exclaimed as he climbed off his bicycle and rubbed a spot on the crossbar shining the bike with a cloth from his pack.

At work she told everyone about their weekend adventure but not about the proposal. "It was so fun."

Terry said, "You hike and bike? But your hair always looks so good."

"What's that got to do with it?" Jo replied.

"I never knew you were an outdoors girl." The traveling nurse replied.

Soon they were talking about Terry's rock climbing and planned to go out Friday to happy hour. Joanna often hung out with the travel nurses who came to staff the hospital for three months at a time. They were the single ones like Joanna without husbands and babies at home.

Another nurse was making gossip at the other bedside Joanna could just tell and she would hear about it later. She would hear that she was spoiled and about her dates and her looks and how great she thought she was. "Don't listen to that." Ellen, a dark-haired Hispanic woman of about 45 said. "Joanna they're just jealous that's all." Ellen was a down to earth woman someone who you knew was honest. Her years had brought her wisdom and she was as practical as she was thoughtful. She had two sons of her own now grown and one was attending college.

Today Ellen and Jo had lunch together. They talked about the new admits, the new residents, and Ellen's son. "We'd better get back now," Ellen said after 20 minutes at the lunch table. "That elevator can take 10 minutes." Then she added, "It's funny, do your friends who watch the soap operas think we are sitting with the doctors and flirting with the surgeons over leisurely lunches in the cafeteria? Some of the ladies at my club think so.

"Yes yes," Jo replied as she laughed.

"But in reality we are rushing to get a bite to eat and a moment of peace," Ellen said as her fingers swept over her rosary beads that tucked into her scrub top, "It's nice that the doctors have their own cafeteria, and sometimes I think we should have our own too."

Joanna stacked her dishes together on her tray. "That would be nice, or with the doctors. Terry would like that. I'm bringing my drink with me. Ready?"

After sleeping in Wednesday, Jo sauntered into the living room and sat with Dancer. She flipped on ESPN to do yoga with the instructor. After that, she'd go for a walk or a bike ride, as usual, to get her energy back. First, she decided to change things around make everything brighter. She removed the pictures from the wall in the hall. She picked flowers from the yard and placed them in the dining room. Wandering into the kitchen she took all the placements to the laundry closet. She looked at books while sitting on a wood bar stool in the kitchen at her granite topped island. She pulled out glassware and ceramic plates. Then she unwrapped the Mexican dish she had bought in Sedona and arranged her wares on the counters. Dancer sat by her waiting to go out for a walk after her stint of days sleeping while Jo worked. "OK girl, let's go."

Joanna new every inch of Troon mountain and walking it was like a sigh of relief to be in the openness. "Voices of ancient speak to me now. Is it I who am stubborn, old-fashioned, spoiled?" She thought of the girls in the NICU and the ones that talked about her. How could anyone see me as spoiled when here I am 30 years old, I have no family, no sisters to talk and go out with, no brothers to help me in a fix, and no mom or dad to advise me and accept me no matter what I do. I wish I could go back and visit. She thought of the peace she felt in the days when she flopped on her parent's couch and drank ice tea with her mom. Her dad would peer in from his office now and then and later squeeze in next to her on the sofa sharing with her a book he was reading or something worldly. There is something special about being with people who know who you really are and accept you. That's home. How nice it was to go home and just be, she thought.

As Joanna recalled family life, there was a scurry a few feet ahead in the brush and Dancer took off quickly at top speed sniffing after a rabbit. "Get him," she called to her knowing Dancer never actually caught one. This was an activity where the pleasure was the journey, the actual chase. Dancer ran circles around a shrub, checked by rocks and underbrush for the rabbit. Soon Dancer reappeared at Joanna's feet and drank from the sports bottle she carried. They turned right at the dip in the road. 'Live together', the words she had heard reappeared, that was something college students did, not a woman of 30. She would have it all, the true heartfelt relationship, the celebration, the family of 2 that becomes in their unity so much more. Her thoughts spinning, she began a slow jogging pace as if to outrun them. She wanted her future to unfold gloriously. She and Dancer ran past Jomax Hills and up to 178th street, where Dixeleta met the dead end. There they circled backstopping to climb up the side of one huge rock jutting 50 feet in the air. She sat and gazed at Four Peaks in the distance with its mountain caps topped with snow like crowns. Where had the time gone? I'm a country girl she said to herself as they climbed down. But you have to be in the city to work. She was still talking to herself as if she had some decision to make. Turning left by the fencing to where the dirt road met the pavement, they soon arrived home.

Joanna gave in and called Sara not sure if she was ready to share everything she felt. "Sedona was beautiful and I biked up airline road do you know what an incline that is! He said he had something special to say."

"And a ring, did he give you a ring?"

"Sara, he wants to live together."

"That's good isn't it? Then you two can move on in this relationship. You have been much too patient Joanna."

"Well, that's just it Sara I was hoping for a ring."

"Of course, you are. He'll get you one, he just doesn't know how to propose. He is planning it."

"Do you think so?"

"Sure"

"Hum, I guess ."

Somewhere in the East

*I*n another state, far from Arizona, the remaining leaves of yellow and orange and gold littered the ground. A little girl sat on the porch step of a gray two-story house with old wood siding. Her name was Katie. It was early afternoon. Before her in the yard, several children played, only one of whom was her sibling. The girl in the red dress, Mandy, was her friend, not her best friend just a friend. Having never learned to trust Katie did not invest much of herself into friendships. She twirled a leaf in her hand. She had found this one leaf yet untrampled. Behind her came a voice "Mandy" the lady called. "Jeff and Todd now don't get dirty. I told you"… and the woman stepped out in front of the little girl to walk down the steps. "Your new parents are coming, Mandy don't you want to look pretty for your trip to your new home?" She brushed Mandy's buttocks and pushed back her bangs off her forehead. "That's better, now honey why don't you swing nicely now." Back up the steps, the woman came and as she did she stopped and bent over to cup the little girls chin. "Katie dear, smile," she said lightly, "It's a beautiful day." Katie moved one corner of her mouth. Satisfied, the foster mother went into the house.

Katie had big brown eyes she also had a temper. But today she was sullen. No one chose her, no one better she thought because daddy's coming. He'll come and find me, he always comes even if he's late, he comes. Her thoughts flashed to several weeks earlier when she had sat, much in the same way, on the steps of her own home on 42 street. She waited for daddy late in the day. Sometimes he was all fun and play. He would carry her about and play football with her and wrestle in the fall leaves. Other days he was late to come home and he would wobble when he walked up the steps. On these days, he looked really tired and he would soon be on the couch falling asleep fast. Mommy worked dinners at the diner and sometimes all night. Katie liked the pie that mommy brought home, it was the best.

One day, daddy did not come home. Mommy had not come home the night before either but it was OK because Katie would walk to school with her older brother Jacob, and take their younger brother to the babysitter just half way down the block as they often did because it was on the way. After school, Katie sat on the stoop feeling disappointed because today she had made a beautiful drawing, and no one came home to see it. She sauntered into the house and the screen door banged behind her. Jacob was at a friend's house. Usually, he would make the peanut butter sandwiches. She climbed up on the counter to get the peanut butter. She had already laid out the bread on the counter for three sandwiches, one for herself and one for each brother. An unfamiliar voice called from the door. She wandered over, peanut butter knife in hand. The lady was from the state and she took her and her brothers away. Now she was with several other kids in the foster home.

Katie twirled the leaf that was in her hand, jumped up, picked up two more she had spotted and put them carefully in her pocket. Walking by Mandy, Katie pushed her and took the small plastic toy figure from her. Soon the two were arguing loudly. The foster mother came out and separated the two just as a car drove up. Katie watched as Mandy was hugged and patted before climbing into the back seat. She had a new home probably with dolls and her own room. Mandy waved to Katie from the back window of the blue Honda Accord. Katie stared, slowly she lifted her hand with her fingers splayed. A tear welled up in her eye. She wiped her jacket sleeve across her face with the other hand. Then she pulled out the leaves walked into the house where a song on the radio was playing. It was one she would sing to sometimes. *"Isn't anybody going to come and find me.... Isn't anybody going to take me home...o... ome.... It's a long cold night...ever going to make it right...."*

The Holidays

*B*rad's family came to visit for the holidays. Arizona was nice this time of year. One day Joanna joined them for dinner and another day they all went touring to Tortilla Flats. On Thanksgiving Day, Joanna had to work as her share of the holidays, but the nurses always made it fun. Jean made a turkey, they used sheets for tablecloths over the tables in the lounge, and everyone brought in a dish. They ate all day long and parents came in to see their babies. The day was warm and wonderful. The next week Jo's group of nurse friends went to lunch and another evening they went to the Hyatt for dinner, drinks and Christmas music.

This month the new residents were coming to intern in the NICU and there was to be a lunch and a reception at the hospital. In the evening, there was a party at the restaurant on East fourth downtown. Everyone from the unit came with husbands, boyfriends and girlfriends. While Brad was mingling with some other people over by the bar, the new pediatric resident, Harry Belmont engaged Joanna in conversation. Joanna responded with introductions. "Have you met Terry? Terry is an RN from Colorado.

She skis, she kayaks!" Harry and Terry enjoyed talking together they both had a fun attitude toward going through life and it's challenges. Terry was always in the moment and Harry seemed very honest and caring. Mary was there with her husband Jeff, and so was Kelly. Barb was with her husband, Lisa with Steve her fiancé, Becky with Tom. Virginia brought her sister, Hilda and Diana showed up and all the spouses and friends and several doctors and new residents had time to be social.

Late into the evening the band played and everyone danced, guys with girls, girls with girls, nurses with doctors and therapists. The funny remark of the evening that nurses made to other nurses and nurses made to doctors and doctors to respiratory techs was "Oh it's you, it's hard to recognize you in clothes!" This was followed by laughter, as most everyone wore loose scrubs and sometimes scrub hats and hair was wild or ponytailed at work. The parties although rare, were really good for morale and in the days that followed everyone at work seemed friendlier. That was the wonderful thing about Christmas Joanna thought.

At Sara's, there was a new addition to the family this holiday, a little girl that was her brother's child was staying with them. Her name was Katie and she was as cute as she was sassy. Her deep brown eyes seemed to hold the weight of the world and her temper was fiery. At eight years old she had been in foster care as Sara's brother was an alcoholic and a drug addict and the wife who had custody had decided she didn't want to be a parent anymore.

"Imagine that, " Joanna said, "how could anyone ever!" Sara was now planning to adopt Katie and Katie seemed to thrive in the busy household. At Christmas, Joanna had gifts for all the kids Katie included. Joanna made time to take Katie for walks and have her over to visit. Spending time together just the two of them, they made brownies and Christmas snowflake ornaments.

Christmas dinner was at Brads house with his mom and his brother and his uncle. There were parties at his finance company and a dinner at the resort on Camelback Mountain which Joanna and Brad went to together. She was hoping for a ring at Christmas but that did not happen. Instead, he bought her a beautiful cashmere sweater from a boutique on one of his business trips to L.A.

Their New Year's celebration was also at Brad's house as his family was still in town and he wanted to have his friends from the hanger come too. Most of them lived closer to Brad or further South. Brad ordered ham and snack trays and Joanna made homemade rolls and together they placed the dishes and candles and ornaments on tables and counters about his house.

Brad's mom having stayed at Brad's for four weeks and his brother having stayed for almost two were now at the Four Seasons with his older brother and his wife and twin boys who flew into town two days before Xmas. At Brad's house, his family was pleased to be chatting with Brad's friends from the hanger about the aircraft. His brother's wife was very nice, she worked in sales. She talked to Joanna about her boys. "My parents spoil them," she said. "But it's just wonderful to have a family. My mom has been watching the boys after school for 2 years now. I don't know what I'd do without her. I think they behave better for her than for me."

Joanna divided her time between the mother and the sister-in-law and the gang from the hanger. She served more food trays as Brad filled everyone's drinks. They played music and some people walked out in the garden and enjoyed the coolness of the evening. His one brother smoked and so they made trips to the patio for smoking. Brad would never let anyone smoke in his house. Joanna also made a lovely dinner and one lunch at her house over the holidays. She loved the holidays but entertaining all his family was at best easier at his place.

The weather was now perfect for hiking. Joann and Brad hiked Troon Mountain and also Pinnacle Peak. They kept a fast pace and talked also as they hiked. Dancer was a welcome hiker at Troon but not at Pinnacle Peak where they had a 'no dogs' sign and park patrol. At the top, there was always time to sit and observe the city below ponder about life's passing moments and share some closeness of their passion for nature.

Also in January, Mary Kelly had her annual art show at the Regency Resort and it was a real elegant affair with a band, wine and hors d'oeuvres. This year it was like a coming out party for her newest style in painting with bronze and silver metallic paints. Joanna and Brad holding glasses of Champaign talked among the guests as they walked Mary Kelly's exhibit. "I love this one with the reds," Joanna said. "It's like a sunset over mountains with the bronze coming up high in the painting glistening at the peak."

"It's my favorite too," said the lady next to her. "A new age style reminiscent of the bronze-age adding depth, like the hope of the future to come."

"The depth of burning knowledge." Another said.

"Wow," said Joanna simply and then to Brad she whispered. "That's the insight you get from appreciating art."

"How do you get all that from a painting?" Brad replied.

"You're really out of your element aren't you if there's no gears or numbers or...." not finishing her sentence, she took his arm and Brad took that as a compliment smiling brightly with his head high. They drifted over to the band and then to Mary Kelly who was chatting with another couple.

Mary Kelly loved it when Joanna was at her party as Joanna was a beauty, a work of art herself and a true friend. "Well there are not many women that are true you know," Mary Kelly said one day as they stood in her studio.

"Yes, all busy at our careers, there's only a few people you can count on like family."

"Don't be so quick about that family stuff, Jo. Not everyone's family is the dreamy group you imagine," Mary Kelly replied that day.

In the resort ballroom, Mary Kelly was talking to a patron... "for a room that size I would suggest you be open to a format of more color... like this one ...." Brad and Joanna trailed about her as she walked the buyer across the room. Then Mary Kelly turned toward them.

"This is my friend Joanna and her... (pause) and this is Brad."

"Nice to meet you," Brad and Jo replied. After some more talk about art, the three stepped to the side and said their good nights.

"Mary Kelly, I am amazed and I must say your work is impressive. It's been a wonderful evening." Brad said.

"Wonderful Mary Kelly." Jo added, "I bet you sell a lot tonight."

"Thank you both so much for coming it's always a pleasure to see you."

"Good night."

On the drive home, Joanna spoke out loud, "I think I'll get that one of Mary Kelly's... Sunset Mt."

"Where will you put it, Jo, in the dining room or the hall?"

"I'm not sure."

"That one is a nice choice, sure you want to spend the money?" And before she could answer he added, "Say what do you say for dinner at Christopher's in two weeks?"

"Ok, something special?" and then she added, "Oh Valentines!"

"Yes, I was thinking about it." He said in a teasing way. "Next week I'm in L.A. on business so it will be a busy week and then I fly back late on Saturday when I'll be getting things together. I'll call you then and see how your weekend is going. We should have our plans down. I'll make reservations."

"Great. Oh, that will be nice. And so you're in L.A.? You're becoming quite the exec, Mr. Walters."

"Thank you, Nurse Styles."

"Well, next Sunday is my weekend to work so I won't be home until 8."

"Then I better not come back injured." They walked in

her front door and Dancer met them. "Jo this house is too big for one. Of course mine, my house," he clarified, "is centrally located." Brad talked easily after a few glasses of wine. He kissed her lips passionately.

"Are you comfortable here at my house Brad?"

"Sure. You put a lot into your house. All the small things, I mean, a bit girly. but it's nice."

She playfully slapped him. Joanna poured sparkling water. "That's so true babe."

They twirled down the hall flipped on music and danced about before climbing into bed to sleep.

Family Life

*I*t was a Wednesday afternoon, Joanna was home and Brad was in L.A. The phone rang at 2pm it was Sara. She was hysterical, kids were screaming and crying and Sara was totally out of her normal mother tone. "Do you need a nurse? What?…is someone hurt?"

"Joann..," Sara's voice was trembling.

"Want me to come over?"

"Yah."

"I'll be right over." She about threw the phone down and ran over in 2 minutes. Sara was holding Janie. Sara's blouse and Janie's face were all blood. Katie was screaming and crying in the hall and Lindsey was quiet and looking scared. Sara shushed them.

"Let me see her. Christ what happened?"

"I've got her Jo, look at her face!" Sara wouldn't let go of Janie.

"Sara! Let go! What happened?" Joanna pulled Janie from her mother's shaking arms.

"No ...She must have fallen after...after Katie, the two of them are always getting into it. Only a minute I went outside and...."

Sara was now crying, she had held on and now that Jo was here she lost it.

"Jo drive us to the ER. Go get Katie," she demanded.

"Let me see her first." She put her on the table. "Get some ice." Now holding pressure and ice on Janie's face, she could see her eye and her lip were cut, her check scratched.

The two women poured water over her face and it spilled over on the table and on to the floor, the towels catching only some. Joanna looked at her with some reassurance.

"Does she need stitches?" Sara asked.

"That near her eye is really just a light scratch but her lip, I'm not sure. I don't know it's a nasty cut. Hold ice on it a minute."

"You go get Katie, Sara, really. I'll hold Janie Bell."

"No, you go. Joanna, I've had it."

"Sara she's new she's scared she needs you." Sara didn't move. "Okay. You stay and hold her, firm pressure here, and ice here."

"I screamed at her, Jo, I slapped her hard."

Meanwhile, Tracy and Lindsey were sitting in the family room.

Joanna walked down the hall. Katie was throwing things in her room. Her arm was scratched and bleeding and she was wild and mad.

"Come here little girl, let Joanna see you."

"No." She screamed as she threw another toy at the wall.

Joanna grabbed her up while Katie was still throwing things and resisting her. On her arm were some bite marks too. Carrying her into the kitchen she said, "Now, now it's OK."

"Don't get them close," Sara ordered. "Really." She screamed at her. "Jo it's not all the Brady Bunch here!"

"Christ, I thought someone drowned or something."

"That 'd be easier."

"Janie bit her, Sara!"

"Yaaah I would've too. Look at her face. She could be scared for life."

Joanna sat Katie down in a chair to tend to her. She began to clean up Katie's arm. "It looks like a war zone in here." Sara and Janie now calmer, sat quietly.

Soon Katie was all betadine and bandaids and saying she hates everyone while still flailing her arms. "Stop it now, how many times have you been to Joanna's house and look you have sisters and a mom who loves you." Crying, Katie rubbed her eyes and then started punching her own chest. "Its OK now, now shush sha," Joanna said as she took the child and rocked her in her arms just like as she did the babies in the unit.

"She's mean and I hate her."

"Shusha sha" Joanna repeated holding Katie tight and rocking her. After a short while, she said, "Will you sit for a minute?" Katie sullenly nodded in agreement.

Joanna got up and moved the cloth Sara was holding. "How's my other patient? Let's see that lip. Now no one is hating anyone."

"She wrecks everything, Auntie Jo." Blood dripped down Janie's cheek when she spoke.

"Ouu, that auntie Jo really gets to me, baby."

"She can't live here anymore, mommy said." Janie cried out and more blood came from her wounds

"Honey I love you but don't talk." Turning to her friend she gasped, "Sara!?"

"I was out in the garage for just a few minutes and they're screaming in here." Sara was now feeling guilty. "She's making me crazy Jo, I can only handle so many kids."

"Sara call your pediatrician and see if he will look at her. Let me talk to him, no, ask if he can suture does he do stitches, Sara?"

"Yah, Tracy's finger."

"Ok, tell them we are coming if they can take us now. You do not want to sit in a hospital ER."

Sara held Janie while Jo took Katie with her to get the car.

They walked across the lawn in the afternoon. Katie said to Jo, "She's a baby, a brat and...."

"Katie," Joann interrupted, "I hope Janie is OK."

"She fell, Joanna."

"And did you push her?".

"I wanted Sponge Bob. I got it first. She bit me."

Jo stopped on the lawn and squatted down to Katie's level looking in her eyes she said, "Katie, Janie is your cousin."

"I'm sorry."

"I'm sure you didn't mean to hurt her. It will be OK now. Let's just be good."

Jo drove over to Sara's.

At the doctor's office, Jo held Katie, and Tracy and Lindsey sat looking a children's books and playing with toys while Sara took Janie in.

When they came out much later Sara was calmer and Janie was holding a small plastic toy. Then the doctor had a look at Katie. On the way home, Joanna stopped at the market. "Just a minute. Katie, come with me." Calling into the car, "Do you have some soda?"

"Four kids Jo, of course, I have soda."

She picked up the prescription, some ointment the Dr. had ordered and while waiting she noticed the first aid shelf and picked out more bandaids & steri-strips for Sara's medicine cabinet as they had used them all. She also got straws, colorful ones and plastic spoons. On the way to the check out she chose some ice cream quickly not wanting Katie to choose it or think it was a reward.

At Sara's, Joanna dished out the ice cream and talked with the girls. Everyone made peace and dared not to misbehave. Then she poured Sara a glass of wine. "Were watching you," she called out to the kitchen table from her chair in the family room.

The ladies talked for an hour, and they laughed finally, agreeing they were probably just as bad when they were youngsters. Just as Jo was getting up Kevin came home.

"Oh, good shift change," Joanna called out sarcastically.

"What?" Kevin responded.

"Relief is here, second shift," Jo said with a smile.

"Shut up," Sara said.

"Bratt," Joanna replied.

"Bye Jo thanks."

The next day Joanna called and checked in with Sara when she got home from work. Sara had decided to let Katie go back to Ohio she had not told Katie yet but the situation wasn't working out. Katie and Janie fought non-stop and even the older daughter, Tracey, was mad at Katie and at her mother. It was also stressing her marriage. "Katie just demands all my time Joanna, and she's got to be the center of attention. You know I love her but I have three other children who are mad at me all the time for bringing her home. She just needs so much. No matter what I give she needs more."

"Let's talk tomorrow, I'm so tired."

"Come over for coffee Jo, please?"

"OK, I'll bring Dancer before we walk."

In the morning, they sat having coffee.

"You spent time with her, you know what I mean."

Joanna did know how she had a temper and wanted all the treats at the zoo or she would pout. She was a little mad and pouty about not getting to buy a stuffed toy and a game at the mall and she said mean things sometimes to Joanna.

"I figured it would all fade away as Katie felt less need to defend herself."

"I thought so too," Sara replied. "I just love her and I thought love would conquer all. I think she's just perfect for one person who has all the time for her. If she was the only child, you know, just for one person...."

"Yeah sometimes with one person ...."

"Ah, you know, (she paused). Jo...."

"For me!"

"Jo how great!" the two women exclaimed as their eyes met in their moment of brilliance, followed by silence.

"Are you sure? Think about it today. I will call the court to see," she said. "But you're not family so it may not be easy."

"Really Sara do you think they would let me without a father for her. Is that fair?"

"Well, you never know how your life will change."

On this morning walk after coffee, all Joanna thought about was Katie and her own desire to be a mom. Can I do it? What will Brad say? It was a beautiful February morning crisp and cool in the desert. The greens were greener and the birds were singing in her neighborhood.

As she walked home, she pictured them doing homework and monitoring TV shows, having a sitter when she went on dates with Brad and then living with Brad, the three of them. In her mind, she thought about decorating the spare bedroom, PTA, clothes shopping, play dates. Joanna made her decision and she was sure. She almost ran home to make the call.

"Sara, call the judge."

"I did Joanna I already called the caseworker. He's looking into it!"

Brad was staying at the Regency in LA in a really nice suite they had reserved for him. After the day's meetings on the second night he walked about the stores and peered into jewelry stores looking at rings. Valentine's Day would be here soon.

By chance, he ran into Mary Kelly's husband in the lobby as he returned. Manny was promoting an art show to be held at the Regency. They talked and decided to have a drink at the restaurant. Brad had a margarita and Manny had a beer. "I've several paintings with me. Also, I carry different artists' portfolios. I make up brochures and save the ones from the most recent show. The hotels really like the business it brings them. This is a great resort. Do you stay here often?" He added.

"I just started coming here. We're opening a branch office. It's the way to do things nowadays."

"I hear you."

"Joanna plans to buy one of the bronze series."

"I have a few here they are going to go fast."

"Really," Brad said thoughtfully stroking his chin.

He had with him the one painting that Joanna liked. "I want to get Jo something special, maybe this is the one. I thought she bought it...."

"Yah man there's only one."

"Now, I can carry this on the plane right?"

"Hey just wink at the attendant, it's going to sell by this weekend."

"She really wanted this. This will be great."

"I'll give a special price Mary Kelly would want that."

"Thanks. When are you driving back, Manny?" They moved to the sports bar for dinner and both ordered beer. Talked about business, watched the game and Brad told Manny about his newest car.

Brad flew back on Saturday after the auto auction. On the airplane, a young woman physician, an allergist, sitting next to him, struck up a conversation with him. She had been visiting her sister in California. She was tall and had dark hair like Brad. They had to deplane onto the tarmac due to some mechanical malfunction. When she stood she was quite elegant, dressed in a short skirt with a small flowered print and a black silk top, her bag was Gucci as were her sunglasses. Her name was Marisa. "Marisa, nice to meet you," she said as they walked toward the gate.

"I guess we're stuck here a while," Brad said as he accepted the drink voucher from the desk attendant.

"Walk with me?" Marisa asked of him as she headed to the café.

"Sure we should go use our tickets and you can tell me about LA." Brad walked by her side as he asked about her family and what she knew about

California. Brad was pleased to be sitting with Marisa. "Beautiful and smart," he commented.

She laughed and steered the conversation back to Phoenix and Brad's personal life. "I see you like art?"

"Oh yes a friend is an artist," he added. "This painting is an original I had to buy it before it was sold."

"I love to go to galleries about in L.A. and in Scottsdale. Do you live in Phoenix?" she asked.

"Yes, I do. My company has plans to expand in L.A. I want to get a feel for the area in case I decide to move there. That's why I was asking you about the area."

"I may move there myself," Marisa said. "I miss my family sometimes and the ocean. It's so nice to live by the ocean. Maybe we should keep in touch. Are you dating?" Marisa added.

"I'm dating a nurse," he admitted. "She's a prenatal nurse with babies."

"You mean neonatal?" Marisa being a doctor corrected him.

"Yes, that must be it." He didn't know the medical words but smiled just the same, proud of his business ventures.

They chatted for a while, their flight was called and they returned to the plane. They were sharing stories on the way back to Arizona when Marisa slipped Brad her card in case he ever had a need for an allergist, she said, or a friend.

While Brad was flying back Katie and Joanna were at Joanna's house making Valentines cards for Katie's classmates. Valentine's Day was next week. They used paper doilies, cardboard, and photos, then they cut them all up. When she returned Katie to Sara' house Sara was pleased. "Thanks for just a bit of free time and anytime to keep these two from fighting. Well, I got the scoop, come in a minute can you? The first person to get her is her mother's sister and she wants to try for custody, although I don't think it will be good for Katie. I think she does drugs. I'm going to oppose it. Then the foster parent that has her brothers has the right to adopt her and that's where they will have to put her at the end of the school year when she leaves us until the sister is cleared. You're not family and so he will put you down on the list."

"Oh," Joanna managed to say.

"There's always a chance Jo," Sara offered. "The foster mom will find out how hard it is to handle two boys and her."

"She's probably married."

"She is and her husband is a teacher."

"Great," Jo said flatly.

Returning home, she went to bed to watch TV, avoiding answering the phone. She set the alarm for 5 am. At work the next day Sunday Joanna was sullen. Then to top it off Lisa handed out wedding invitations. Mary announced her second pregnancy, adding she had met her goal of having her children before age 35. Joanna was happy for Lisa and joined a few of the girls who could free up their assignments for lunch, in the cafeteria. Outwardly she laughed and chatted with her friends, but really she was disappointed about the idea that she may not be the one for Katie. Life, she thought, was supposed to flow much more easily.

After work she lay on the couch dozing, the ringing phone brought her around. "Hello"

"Hi there how's my Jo? Sunday night …."

"I'm tired."

"You're tired, I had the longest trip. We stayed at the … and I think the manager in LA thinks…. I know what I'm doing… it's funny cause… I'm just really calm and…."

Joanna listened as she always did but tonight she heard only every other word.

"And George what does he say?"

"He's kind of funny one day he's … but I told him…."

"OK, well great I'm going to sleep now. Did you miss me?"

"Yeah Jo, how's Dancer?"
"She's fine …chasing rabbits"

"Ok then good night."

Valentines Day

*J*o stayed in on her days off this week. She sat on the patio played sad songs and hip songs and rock. Katie was leaving and she had hoped to be someone special in her life. Katie certainly had become part of Joanna's life. She was happy that for Katie there would be aunts and foster moms. Maybe she would get to visit Sara in the summer and play with her cousins. Yes, Joanna had gotten carried away with the idea she would be a parent and get to take Katie shopping, and skating and teach her to fly kites. There was so much more to do too and so many things to come in a little girl's life. It was just not meant to be she decided, and it hurt.

Wednesday Brad called to confirm weekend Valentine's dinner. Saturday he arrived at Joanna's house and he was pleased to see her in a flowing red dress with the scoop neck. Its delicate skinny straps accentuated her slender shoulders. "Jo, you look wonderful.!"

Jo smiled. "Thank you and so do you Brad" she replied as he stood grinning wearing a new shirt.

At Christopher's they parked using a valet and after stepping inside the restaurant Brad ran back out to check on something. So like him, Jo thought, always so concerned about his car. As she waited she gazed about the room at the furnishings and the people arriving for dinner. They sat at a booth on the side of the room and ate oysters, as they sipped wine. They ordered salmon and steak and asparagus, and for dessert Crème brûlée. With their wine glasses full they toasted to love and to success. "Oh isn't this nice?" Brad remarked. "Here's to us."

Dinner arrived shortly. "And for you Madame the salmon."

"Thank you."

They ate and talked and just before dessert arrived the waiter came over with a large package. "I believe this is yours."

Brad smiled and Joanna looked puzzled. "Happy Valentine's Day Jo."

"Brad!, What did you do? Oh, it must be... well, Oh Brad!" Joanna fussed as he gave her the gift of art. "I love it! How did you get this? You are so sweet to remember. I always need more art! She admired the painting wondering how he must have planned so well to have the valet bring it in from the car. After thanking him, she reached into her purse and brought out a tiny package. She had bought him a new iPod.

"If they make them any smaller I'll lose this one too." He said smiling. "Thanks, Jo, this is a great sweetie," and he leaned over and kissed her on the lips. They toasted to love and success. They talked about Mary K's art show and his trip to San Fran and her looking for a gift just right for him. They talked about beaches in San Fran and how nice it would be to live near the ocean. Joanna asked about the sea otters in the harbor, the artists, and Brad talked about the restaurant he ate at with his company associates.

All the while dining, looming over her was the fact that Katie would be moving back to Ohio. Thinking of her Jo said, "Remember you said about a year ago how you wanted a little girl?"

"Jo but my career, now, I mean you know I'll be traveling more now with this office in LA. I mean I may have to move. When the company decides these things you don't have a choice. Is this about the painting?" Brad had been so pleased with himself was Joanna going to push him about having children?

"The painting? I love the painting it was so thoughtful. I can't believe you knew exactly which one!" And again he was proud of himself.

Brad began to tell the story of how he ran into Manny at the Regency.

When he was done Joanna said, "Well I wanted to ask you," she paused. "I'm taking Katie to pizza next Friday night. Want to join us?

"Sure."

They finished dinner and then they went to Brads house in town and fell into bed both tired from their long week and soon were asleep.

That next Friday Brad met them for pizza in Tempe at a little place Joann used to frequent and later she and Brad had been there with friends on Fridays and sometimes Sundays.

Katie told Brad how she made cards with Joanna and about her friends at school. Brad said he would take her to the hanger to see the planes someday. Brad played the pinball and computerized games along the wall with Katie. They laughed and shouted as each of them scored points and Joann was very pleased with this scene before her. He was great with her. They all sat down ate pizza and a great time.

Joanna buckled Katie in her car to drive her home. Brad followed in his car close behind them. Once in the neighborhood, Brad stopped at Joanna's house while Joanna drove Katie around the corner to Sara's. "She was Great." Joanna said.

"Yeah? Thanks, Joanna. She loves her dates with you." Sara said as she snuggled Katie putting her hand around the little girl and resting it on her shoulder. "Bye bye"

"See ya."

Joanna drove home. "I'm back."

Brad's comments were positive. "We can take her out again if you like." I like how she looks you in the eye. "She's a great little girl."

Joanna smiled, he did have a spot for children. "Wine?" Jo said and turned about to the kitchen and he followed her. They opened the wine and filled their glasses taking them to the bedroom.

Brad went for the TV and Jo followed him. Sliding her hand down his arm she put the remote back and instead reached for the CDs.

"Classics or rock?"

They danced a slow dance and while doing so he unzipped her dress, pulled off his dress shirt and pulled her close to him. They stood Victoria Secret to Ralph Lauren, she in red he in black. She kissed his chest as he unhooked her bra and it fell to the ground. Their lips met and they kissed over and over drinking in their closeness. "You're just right for me," he said now fluffing her hair that fell about her back and shoulders. She slid her bare leg between his legs and they lay back on the bed. With their legs intertwined they rolled over and as they made love it seemed more special to Joanna. They were more than lovers and friends, they were partners and would someday be parents and husband and wife. It was all so perfect or it would be. Together they moved and breathed and with their eyes closed they sighed loudly then winking their eyes open they gazed deep into each other's eyes. They became one with each other and the universe. Pleasantly tired now, she lay on his chest her slender frame and soft breasts pressed into his firm chest. His hand stroked her naked body while still holding her. As he admired the curve of her hip he said ..."Jo? Would you ever live in LA?"

"I don't know maybe"

"It's right by the ocean and I know you love the ocean …" he was drifting in his tiredness.

"I love …walking on the beach," she whispered. And they drifted off to sleep.

In the morning, Brad and Jo went to the gym. She worked on her machines of choice as he did his and later they would meet somewhere in the middle and watch each other. Brad liked to give Jo pointers and Jo liked to oh and awe at Brad's muscles teasing him. On many occasions, Jo would meet Terry at the other gym near the hospital to play volleyball with their hospital team. It was the whoever shows up kind of team and it was always fun.

That night, they went to dinner at Oaxaca for Mexican food. Terry and her date met them. "It's great up here in the North Valley, so pretty."

"I love it."

"You're so spoiled."

"I know. So you live in Brad's neighborhood I think." Joanna said turning to Peter.

They talked about houses and neighborhoods and nurses and doctors, being on call, and such polite subjects. Terry's date, Peter, was an administrator from work. They had met when Terry helped herself into the doctor's cafeteria. "Well they have better food and I was lost, yeah that's it lost." They laughed.

Peter and Brad talked cars and then they all talked current events.

Sunday, the next morning, at Jo's house it was a lazy day. They turned on sports and flipped through the paper. Joanna had a stack of mail to go through. Over juice and coffee, she opened a card and read the paper. She pulled out the jewelry ads "Umm Um Hum" she said as she tugged at the paper dropping it in front of Brad.

"Looks like rings. I'm just not sure."

"Sure?

"Well, I have ...."

"You have what Brad?"

"Well, I like things the way they are."

"You said you want to live together, you mean just for the heck of it?"

"No to see you more."

Now teasing she said, "Well that's a blessing you mean every other weekend or so isn't bliss?"

"Joanna, I said I wanted to live with you. You know I.. you know... we are. Well, I guess we could look."

Joanna smiled. "Yea!"

"Too bad it's Sunday."

"Sunday?"

"They're closed. Maybe next week." And he returned his gaze to the newspaper section he was holding.

"Brad Walters."

It was a few weeks later April 5 Katie's Birthday and the two went to Sara's house to her party. "Hey Kevin," Brad greeted Kevin.

"Long time no see Brad"

"Come on in." Inside they went into the great room and sat on the bar stools. Kevin made drinks. "Margaritas or beer?"

Sara took her time at coming over to sit with Joanna. "We found out Katie's other relative gets her. They called yesterday morning to wish her happy birthday. I'm sorry Jo for both of you I know she'd be better with you, but I'm beat, I'm worn out."

"Hey, it's OK."

"She doesn't know yet, we're waiting until the school year ends to tell her."

"Let's go out to the barbecue," Kevin hollered out to Brad who was standing there looking awkward. The two men stopped at the kitchen counter to pick up plates of hot dogs and hamburgers and some grilling utensils. "These are my best tools, best for grilling and keeping me out of the girly talk. We will miss her. I just think we have enough to handle, and our children are not adjusting as we hoped. I hate to sacrifice the whole family."

"I know Kevin. I have enough with work and we are getting more work from California."

"Yeah?"

"Well, it seems like they're not enough people in California and we're slow enough here with work that we can take it on, add it to our practice."

"Is there a promotion in your future?"

"That would be great. They know I am always there, always staying late and I get things done."

"Daddy I want a hot dog," Lindsey said as she ran up to him and hugged her arms around his waist while leaning her head back and looking up at his face.

"How many dogs, Sara?" Kevin hollered out with Lindsey still attached to his legs. He patted her affectionately. "Having fun pun-kin?"

The children and adults mingled and played games. The women brought out chips and carrot sticks and salads and later everyone ate cake after Katie, of course, blew out all the candles.

Later when the other guest have gone home the four adults sat in the back yard and watched the sunset over the mountains while the kids played in the house. Joanna tells Brad she was hoping to adopt Katie. Sara adds that she would be a great mom and Brad agrees adding that it would be tough to be a single mom. That one comment he made stuck in Joanna's mind.

It was a fun Saturday that turned into a late night with grown-ups having drinks by the pool while the kids watched movies in the house. They drank as they wished as Joanna's house was only a short walk away. After they said good- bye for the evening they stepped outside onto the front porch. "She's pretty smart huh?" Joanna ventured.

"Still Jo she's someone else's kid and I don't believe in that" Brad replied as they walked home.

"Well, there's not much chance to get her anyway." And with that, the conversation was over.

The next Saturday morning was not starting out well. Joanna and Brad were standing in the kitchen at Joanna's house and they began to argue. Joanna had been invited to a friends wedding at work and now Brad said he was not going to be able to go with her as there was a car auction that weekend in San Francisco.

Joanna cried. "I told you about this weeks ago. You're not going?" She stopped moving about and looked him in the face. "One day you're going, the next you're not, you like me, you don't like me, you like kids, you don't want kids. What's with you? What about us? It's been almost 2 years. I just can't do it anymore. How long can I compromise and wonder what your plans are? Don't you know what you want in a person, in a girlfriend by this age?" She avoided saying wife. "It's like it's all about you! You and your car, you and flying the planes, your football team, you and your hair for god's sake wake up. Are that car and the plane really going to make you happy five years from now, what about ten." Joanna was not herself or maybe she thought, of being out of control, that she was more herself, not so passive and pleasing.

"What am I to you the girl next door, your slut? Just a Friday fling, well I'm not doing this anymore." One day he seemed ready to propose and talk about their future and the next it was like it never happened, at least like it was just kind of figuratively speaking. "I have goals and I have plans and you are not meeting them. Your selfish Brad just selfish and now it's going to be summer soon and then fine, you just go on and go fly off to San Francisco to see your Uncle and do whatever it is you two do. I don't need a ring or a promise from you. Just forget it I don't want to marry you anymore. We have Lisa's wedding to go to and I'm going." Joanna started to cry and Brad approached her. She hit him hard and flat on the chest with the palm of her hand twice. Again she raised her arm but he caught it midway. "You stupid man she cried."

"Jo" Brad looked shocked and sad at the same time. He became quiet. He was too quiet for Joanna. His face now sullen and pale he suddenly looked older than his 34 years.

"Braad" Joanna wined, "it's over isn't it, it's just over."

"No Jo I don't see us as over. Don't give up on us he implored her." His face flushed and his eyes were red and watery.

"I'm just a little slow. I was thinking we could live together, do this thing gradual Joanna....'

Joanna laughed in her tears "live together, oh that's just great and for little Janie and Lindsey we'll set a great example. You know I can't live with you. I thought we were going to be engaged and planning our wedding."

"So what about them they're neighbor kids."

"They're part of Sara's family and she's as close to me as if she was my sister. It's what I want, not her, not anyone else it's about how I feel. I just won't feel proud. How is it so different for you that you can't commit, don't you love me?" Joanna was now bargaining. She'd gone from her power position, of standing for what she wanted, to that need to be needed in his plans. They sat and talked for a long time and nothing really was accomplished except that Joanna was heard and Brad was there to do the hearing and so calming her by his mere presence and listening.

Joanna stood up. "Well I've got a million things to do now," Joanna said not wanting to talk, to play this game. She didn't need all this. She wanted to have a nice day, to just have a normal life. Looking at Brad, abruptly she said, "Don't you have things to do?"

"Jo I'll go. I'll rearrange things. I've things to do but let's have dinner later."

"No."

"I'll call you."

"Don't force yourself."

"You know I think about you all the time. We'll work it out, Jo. Tonight Jo... we'll go to Christopher's for your favorite southwest salmon."

"Well, I don't feel like GOING To Christopher's..."

"Then we'll go to Oaxaca and drive in the convertible, you'll like being out. Come on Joanna."

She just looked at him.

"I'll call you." He said.

Joanna paused and looked up. Her anger had dissipated; for once it should be all about me she thought. "I'm sorry I hit you."

"Oh that, that was nothing, really hey you've been frustrated with this for so long I think it's just built up in you."

It was so nice to hear him say that and with that, she felt understood. He took her hand pulled her close and kissed her on the cheek before he walked out the front door.

Later in the day she walked the neighborhood. The time to be out was now while it was spring and the weather was nice. She met the neighbors at the park at the end of the block. Margaret, who had a lab like Dancer and Nancy who lived a few doors down were there. She rarely saw Nancy except when her little Jack Russell dog would run toward Jo's house and she'd come over to retrieve it quickly.

As the dogs ran about and some children threw balls across the park, the three women talked. The conversation went from dogs to marriage. Jo attempted to congratulate Nancy as she heard she had married this last fall and Nancy replied they'd already divorced, hardly worth the effort. Jo was shocked. "Well, he never worked... I don't know, he didn't take care of the yard either. He never could find the right job," Nancy said.

Margaret agreed. "It's hard to find a good man. I'm on my second marriage my first was only a year. I learned allot after that. About myself I mean. It seems it doesn't matter if you get married or not you can still break that commitment."

"I guess if it's not a promise from the heart," Joanna replied.

The talk at the park changed Joanna's mood and so when Brad called she talked freely. Jo decided to accept his offer and dress for dinner. She chose a sheer summer dress in pink with a low cut neckline and skinny straps. She put on her favorite Cartier platinum earrings and the pearl bracelet that was once her mother's adorned with the Tiffany heart she had added to it. Brad arrived wearing a Tommy Bahama linen shirt in white and silk trousers in soft camel.

At dinner, they drank Chateau Polly Fuse and enjoyed a South Western fare at Christopher's of salmon and asparagus with the salsa she so adored. They finished the meal by sharing sorbet. The jazz was a nice change and their mood was brighter. "So what do you think Jo? We can do this. He said as if to convince himself. He took her hand and looked into her eyes. "I do love you my Jo. What do you say?" She almost choked, staring wide- eyed she held back. Was he now on her terms? What of marriage, what about what the girls said in the park?

"What are you saying?" she said, as she sipped her wine and smiled.

"How about some karats... say three?" Her eyes brightened.

The music was playing ... 'there is you and me and all the other people and I don't know why I can't take my eyes off of you... Joanna smiled. He kissed her and they got up to dance. They both enjoyed the evening and their friendship and he talked about LA and the new business. The evening was wonderful, surrounded by jazz and fine food. As their arms encircled each other so did their hearts. They danced to two slow songs and one fast song and laughed. The restaurant was alive. They met a couple at the next table with whom Joanna worked with the husband. He was a doctor in the NICU. After introductions, they spoke briefly and shared a toast to the band. The band received much applause from the dinner crowd that night. Later, Joanna and Brad walked out of the restaurant the energy of joy illuminated them in their new found commitment. He held her for a moment on the porch of the restaurant and together they paused breathing in the night air and gazing at the starry sky. The valet brought the car around and opened the door to his Mercedes E 320, the one he drove to work, "Madam?" and they both got in. Together they rode under the moonlit sky through Phoenix rising from the city lights to the mountain heights.

Later at Joanna's in the height of lovemaking Joanna giggled and Brad sighed. He pulled her onto his chest, "Joanna, my Joanna" Brad sighed. They slumbered peacefully that night, she in his arms, their hearts close beating together.

When Sunday morning came they showered together and then while Joanna fixed her hair Brad took Dancer out. Often when he stayed over he would take Dancer to the wildlife area at the end of the street and have a run. Once dressed, Joanna fluttered around the house like her fish in their aquarium she picked up things that were out of place. She made breakfast and put it out on the patio table. Brad and Dancer would soon be back from their short walk. She set out juiced grapefruit juice she had gotten from her trees, waffles from the freezer and made some scrambled eggs. The sun was already warm as they had slept in. Brad smiled as he let himself in the back gate. "Joanna what a great day."

"It is," Joanna replied. "Let's eat."

At the table, Brad spoke first.

"I can sell my house Jo in two months I could be free and clear. I wanted to tell you earlier. There's a new guy at work and it's just right so I'm thinking it's time we move on and try it. How about sharing your life with me in L.A."

"In L.A. or Arizona? What are you proposing?"

"Jo let's move forward"

"And L.A.?"

"It's near the ocean and it's not for sure"

"I…"

He had worn her down. With his arms around her

now, he said, "I love you, Jo." As they sipped an iced cappuccino at the patio table, he continued. "You are my best friend."

She had been thinking all wrong, he would never say live together against after that fight they had. How silly I have been.

"Will you move to L.A. with me?"

"Yes, you're my best friend too, Brad, I love you."

Jo had a tear.

"What's wrong Jo?"

"Nothing, I don't want to leave."

"We'll make it work, come to L.A. with me."

"And Dancer, Mikey, Yodel and the fish?"

"Yes, the fish too. Hey Jo, after we eat let's go. I have to run some errands."

"Together?"

"Yes."

They went to the wholesale store and bought things. They went to Brad's and dropped off some things and then went back out. "Let's have a sandwich at the corner deli and then drive down Scottsdale road...." Brad looked at her... "to the jewelers."

She smiled.

They stopped at the jewelers. Joanna was thrilled. She tried on rings and they picked their favorites. She liked blue stones with diamonds and he liked the traditional solitaire. She liked the Princess cut and he liked the three stone setting. "We have to think about it. We need to shop around it's always good to think about it and be sure it's the right one."

Spring into Summer

*B*rad was out of town this weekend and Jo was working in the unit. She and Terry, the traveler nurse, had become really good friends. They were both on the admit team the last few weeks and worked together well. Jo liked Terry's easy style nothing seemed to ruffle this girl's feathers. Saturday the one baby had had his heart monitor ringing and an abnormal rhythm strip that scared Jo. "The heck?" she said out loud, and then "I've got a level 2 bed 12," she called over her intercom. The little guy at less that a day old had a heart attack. It turned out the mom had been a crack user. Terry was at the bedside. She only raised her eyebrows yet later she admitted she was as freaked out as Jo. The two stopped at the bar for snacks and a glass of wine after work still in their scrubs yet it didn't matter as this club was next to the sport club where they played racket ball and residents had memberships and played basketball and so it was not unusual to see someone casually dressed having a salad or a burger or a drink.

The DJ was playing dance tunes as the girls chatted with the bartenders. Terry got silly and kept untying the bartender's apron when he got near the end of the bar, as they were sitting on the end where the counter meets the walk through. They later got up and joined the dance group to dance the Macarena. "What the heck Jo."

When they returned, Harry the pediatric resident was at the bar in gym clothes ordering a burger. "Hey, what's up Doc?" Terry said all smiley.

Harry was always nice to Joanna and Terry said it was obvious that he still had a crush on Joanna.

"Hi you two."

"Hey, Harry and Terry my two best buds."

"Very funny."

"Hey come on let's dance."

"I just ordered my burger"

"OK, you're off the hook."

"Terry, did you ever travel to L.A.?"

"Why?"

"Just wondered."

"No, but Mary Beth did."

"Did she like it?"

"I guess, ask her yourself."

"Are you going back to Colorado?"

"I don't know."

"Do you miss it, I mean wasn't it home?"

"I can always go back. I like to see things you know like the Grand Canyon and the river...."

"Hey, you girls want another drink, I'm buying?" Harry interrupted.

"Harry?"

"What of it?"

"Mr. '88 Chevy."

"Hey, that hurt."

"WE love you, Harry," Terry said.

"Heck, my car's 6 years old," Jo added.

"Chardonnay?"

"Two."

"So don't you chicks dig my car. I thought we'd go for a cruise after," Harry said sarcastically.

"We're waiting on that graduation day," they chimed in.

"... and your new SUV." Terry added, "a girl can't be too careful in this part of town. Your car breaks down and its ugly."

"Well I have no debt and not everyone can say that hey miss Terry?"

"Hey, I pay my bills."

"When I start at the Children's hospital I start fresh no loans to repay no worries no debts."

"I like that about you Joanna said. It's a commitment to your work and to life. I have nice things but I don't have to have everything."

"My neighbors have to get the new summer dishes the colored coolers and floats and I guess I got used to just paying for myself you know."

"And your big house..." Terry added.

"Well that's my one thing and I deserve that and you guys know I'd trade it in a heartbeat to have my parents back."

It was Terry who spoke next. "Well, Jo it is... ah... what better place to have a party? I vote for a party at your house."

"And what are we celebrating?"

"Easter?" Terry said searching for an excuse. "Hey, I like how you guys hide the plastic eggs in the unit that is a cool idea Mary showed me the plastic eggs she got at Target. So we hide them for nights and nights hides them for us on days, right? I think we could paint some too. What about the babies will we make shirts for them like we did at Christmas?" Feeling her wine, Terry was going on.

"Do you like living so far away Joanna?" Harry said.

"It's a drive but only three days a week." Joanna replied.

"Yah, I guess if you're not on call."

"Well I'm on call. I'm just ready to go and also ready to be canceled for the day. Sometimes I'm already here and they counted wrong and ask me to go home"

"I hate that," Harry said.

"Me too I mean we're always running our butts off why not keep an extra person on when they count wrong?" Terry added.

"Political bitches."

"Jo I never heard you …."

"Well it's true the little clicky girls think they are hot," Joanna said.

"Really Jo," Harry commented.

"Oh shit." Terry chimed in. "Every unit with 100 or so women has clicks. What do you expect Harry?"

"I guess I don't notice."

"Oh yeah, they talk about Joanna like she's someone she's not, it's just because she's pretty, no gorgeous."

"Shut up."

"Its true," Ellen said, "so how they snipe and you know we cuties have to stick together." Terry said with a smile.

"They're jealous," Harry said

"Yep," said Terry. And adding herself, she said, "The brunette cat woman and the blonde bombshell."

Jo laughed.

"So let's have a party at your house come on Jo, is that pool of yours warm enough?"

"Maybe soon, I can just put the solar cover on."

"Hey that sounds great."

"Speaking of home, I've got an early morning, and I've got a long drive."

"Yeah, East L.A." Terry chimed in "Let's walk out." she added as they set their drinks down.

Now in the parking lot, they continued. "Are you going to make it home in that car?" Terry said to Harry.

"Hey, I don't live far."

"Of course, you don't. You're in the low rent district and you have to take the call. Say where are all the other docs tonight?"

"Probably home in bed."

Then Terry and Harry stood with their arms over

each other's shoulders and began singing an old Bob Seager song, *Born in the USA*, with their own new words as Jo stepped into her car. "I was born in East L.A.... Bye Jo, nice drive."

Off she went first hanging her head out the window singing born in East L.A. back to them and she laughed.

"Is she ever going to marry that guy or do you think she'd dump him for a date with me?"

"Harry I thought I was your true love."

They laughed, "Miss world traveler, you sit still long enough for me to be an established physician?"

"She seems like she's going to wait for him."

"I don't know what is taking him so long," Harry said.

The following week the botanical garden had it's last Jazz in the Garden event for the season and Jo was there both as a speaker and a guest. The evening began with a walk thru the gardens where all the desert plants were marked with signs. At the end of one path, there was a greenhouse with seedlings and the moisture loving plants. Winding thru the gardens at one end was a snack bar and shop where one could buy art and plants and books and such. At the amphitheater, a band set up to play jazz music and Joanna and some other speakers gathered to plan their presentation. The sun set and the stars came out the night sky was beautiful. Manny, Mary Kelly, Sara, Terry and Kevin and Brad sat in the front rows.

"Thank you all for your support to make this wonderful place a place for not only us to enjoy, but for the preservation of the plant life and the wildlife refuge it has become to many animals," Joanna said ending the speaker portion of the night's presentations.

Everyone clapped and Manny who was there with Mary Kelly and being the cowboy that he was hollered out "a toast to Joanna and to the wildlife." Everyone raised their glasses and clapped. Joanna took her seat next to Brad. They spent the night listening to jazz and sharing conversation with the group of volunteers, visitors, guests and neighbors at the patio tables clustered together drinking from crystal glasses. The jazz band played under clear skies, while some folks chatted others walked the grounds guided by the lighted paths.

As the days became warmer school year came to a close. Katie was to leave and Brad was moving into

Joanna's house. Sara and Joanna decided to take Katie on a special girls shopping trip and get her a summer wardrobe at Nordstrom. That's what they told her but they were also wanting to send her off with some nice thing that she might not otherwise get. Joanna showed up at Sara's at 9 a.m. as planned. Katie came to the front door. "Hi, auntie Jo."

"Hi, sweetie."

"Did you know I'm going to Ohio?"

"Yes, I did."

"Doesn't the Judge know how much fun I'm having here?"

"Well yes he does, and the Judge knows that you and Janie fight all the time."

"He does?" Katie replied.

"Well, you sure are a world traveler. Will you be with your little brother Scott?"

"Yes, Jacob and Scott."

"It's cold in Ohio and it snows doesn't it?" Joanna added.

"Yeah," the little girl replied.

"Well, that's why we have to go shopping. I understand you need some new clothes!" Joanna said tickling Katie in the ribs. Katie giggled and smiled and that made Joanna feel good.

They all went to the Scottsdale fashion mall and it was Sara who was having a fling. They went to Nordstrom, Neman Marcus and to the little girl's store All About Clair. They bought sandals and embroidered jeans and designer tops and at Clair's they bought barrettes and silly things like notepads, a stuffed animal, and photo album.

They had burgers at Tommy Rocket's and Katie played the old-fashioned jukebox and got to pick the songs. It was her day and she reveled in the attention.

"Movies!" Joanna cried as they left the restaurant. "OK Sara?"

"What the heck let's do it up right." Sara was so over feeling guilty. Shopping for Katie made her feel better knowing that Katie would have some nice things.

The movie was about a young teen who became a singer. By 4:30 they were all ready to go home and they did. They rolled into Sara's house and plopped on the couch. "Margaritas please," Jo said to Sara's husband.

He laughed, "Hey I've been here with three girls and daddy O is the best daddy. Say right girls?"

"Daddy took us to lunch and ice cream." the girls chimed.

"He did? You mean out for lunch and ice cream." Sara corrected her daughter.

"What did you buy mommy?"

"Well remember Katie is going on a trip so she needs some things."

"I have new sandals and hiking boots." Joanna bought the hiking boots. She thought it would get the foster parents off in the right direction.

"Let's see. I wanna see." The girls went off to the family room.

"Margaritas ladies? Sara where's the glasses?"

"Men. You know Kevin, the second shelf."

"Hey, I'm a beer and scotch man...and ice cream." He added with a smile.

They talked together for a while. Jo finished her drink, said goodbye, and left to walk home.

"Bye, Bye," the girls called at the front steps."

While the ladies were shopping, Brad was making his home at Joanna's unpacking some things in the office Jo had given him to have space of his own. "Hey, How was the mall?" Brad said greeting Joanna.

"Wild, I'm a bit tired. I bought some Coach sandals for me!"

"Yeah?"

"And some things for Katie. We found these cute little embroidered T's and she liked the ruffled tops." Joanna sat in the chair. "She's going Brad she's really going." Her look became sullen.

"Well, you knew this would come."

"I know."

"Now come sit with me check and out the new office," he said as he took her hand and walked her past the living room to the office where Brad had been unpacking.

"Oh, it looks good."

"Say how about some Easter candy to cheer you up?"

"I'm candied out," Joanna said as she surveyed the room. The bookshelves were neatly stacked with his books on finance and business. There were two leather chairs one big armchair at the desk and one across the room with brass rivets along the edges. The rich mahogany desk was adorned with had brass handles on the drawers. On his desk were packages of candy.

"Yeah Look at these chocolate eggs and I got your favorite, Ghirardelli...."

"Oh, Brad."

"and some jelly beans for the kids," he said, as he opened the bag and began eating some.

"You mean for you." She said dropping into the leather chair opposite his.

"Hey, a little sugar is good for everyone."

"What's got into you today?"

"Sugar in the morning sugar in the evening, be my little sugar...." he sang.

"Did your mother teach you that?"

"Joanna come on and have some candy. Look I even picked up those colored plastic eggs for your nursery hunt."

"You did? That was nice."

"I got the pastel ones. The cashier said they open. I hope that's what you like. Open this one."

"Yes, we put stuff in them at work."

"Jo is pink your favorite or would you rather have a jelly bean?" He toyed with the candy intently.

"Ok, I like the orange ones." He tossed her a jelly bean and they both began laughing. He then tossed her the bag. She ate an orange jelly bean and reached in for more.

"I can't open these plastic eggs how do you do it?" Brad said as he handed her a pink egg.

"Let me show you," she said and she rose from her chair and came across the room to sit on him in his big leather chair, "like this." Turning each half a different direction she opened the egg and then with a quick breath in she gasped. "Ahh! My ring, Brad! Brad, it's perfect!"

"You like it, Jo? It's 3 karats. Do you like the..."

"It's beautiful, Oh its sooo nice." Joanna's smile

was as wide as it could be. Brad was beaming too. He had made his decision and that was for him the big step. "I love it."

"Jellybean?" was Brad's comment.
"You silly." Joanna laughed

"Let's see." He said as he took it and placed it on her finger, "a perfect fit."

"You are Brad Walters you are."

They awoke with the sun and turned to each other winking their eyes open. She gazed over at him, he was in her bed and not just for the weekend.

"Joanna are you awake?"

"Sundays are for sleeping in."

"Not today I'm going to the gym."

"Before breakfast?"

"That will take too long, I also want to take the Mercedes SLK to get washed before it's late."

"I thought you were selling that one. Isn't that the '97?"

"Maybe I'll play with it a little longer."

Looking at her hand Joanna said, "Sure Brad I've got stuff to do."

She was dying to show Sara her ring and Sara with 4 kids now rarely slept in. Dancer, let's go little girl. Dancer was always at her side of the bed. When she put her feet down she had to ask Dancer to move. "We're going for a walk OK girl?"

Joanna rang the bell at Sara's house.

"Hey come on in, I'm doing clothes. Come in the laundry room."

Joanna stood with her hand in her pocket.

"It's going to be the same kind of summer," Sara said as she folded a towel. "Hot and...."

"Oh no much different," Jo replied as she pulled her hand from her pocket and played delicately with her necklace. Sara looked at her. "I'm going to be busy with packing and traveling."

"Travel?" Sara echoed.

"Yes!"

"Did you hear about the travel position?"

"I put a few applications out. I guess it's time." She paused still running her finger back and forth toying with her necklace. "You know, see the world. I've yet to ah...."

"Wait!" Sara exclaimed when she looked up from the basket of clothes. Reaching for Joanna's hand, "What's this?. A rock! Let me see!!! YOU Bratt!"

"Ahh!"

"Ahh!" The two women chimed in together.

"Isn't it great?"

"Oh, Joanna it's you. So did you go to dinner last night or what? I just was with you yesterday. She paused. "You're not going to move are you? Tell me Jo I want all the details."

"It was in the egg."

"The egg?" The women wondered into the great room and the kitchen Sara toting the laundry basket.

They sat on the iron bar stools in Sara's kitchen while Joanna told Sara the story and they admired her ring. Sara folded the last of the towels placing them in a neat pile. Then she jumped up and handed Jo an empty coffee mug and a crystal wine glass. "Try this." Jo held each one with her left hand before setting them down on the granite countertop. They laughed as Joanna waved her hand through the air. The two of them were waving their hands now doing the princess wave used in parades. "Elbow elbow, wrist wrist." They were saying in unison as Kevin walked in from the yard.

"What are you ladies doing? Hi, Joanna."

"Good morning."

"Look at Jo's ring Kevin."

"Oh, nice. Congratulations"

A voice came from around the corner. "Mommy?" It was Lindsey.

"This is what comes next," Sara said. "Hi, Baby girl." And with that, she placed her arm around her daughter and pulled Lindsey close to her.

When it came time to go to work Joanna wasn't sure if she should wear her ring or not. With all the moving about of things and washing of hands. She didn't want to lose it. Some nurses pinned their rings to their scrub tops and others didn't wear their diamonds. Still other nurses wore so much jewelry it was a wonder they could work. Well at least for one day, she'd wear it to share her news with the other nurses.

Joanna called Terry and told her about her news. They both had the same day off this week and met to go hiking at Piestewa Peak. They climbed for 30 minutes to reach the top passing some other hikers who were taking it slow. At the top of the mountain, they sat to enjoy the expansive view of the valley. "There's Camelback over east and see Pinnacle Peak off to the North?"

They started talking about work and the heavier NNP who always yelled at them. "Oh, Terry she snaps at everyone," Joanna said reassuring her.

"Her pants are too tight that's what's making her crotchety," remarked Terry. And Joanna laughed.

"What's her name?"

"Oh, a Mmm no sss something I don't know right now."

"So she walks by and says to me -What are you doing taking out the staples of that kid's head? I hope you have an order for that!"

"Really?"

"I wanted to say well gee there, Humpty Dumpty I had nothing better to with my time so I thought I'd rip these out."

"Humpty Dumpty! HA HAA Ah Ha Ha." Joanna was rolling on her side. "You don't call her that Terry, do you?"

"Yah in my head. With that hair cut I think she looks like Humpty Dumpty."

"She does! She does," Joanna laughed.

Terry started laughing too. "I'd never say that Jo you know even though she's mean to me."

Joanna was holding her stomach. "How about the other one Roxanne?"

"What?"

"She came to my bedside one day and I said I think I need to go up the vent rate, and she looked at me and said something about not telling her what was what and I said we just need to work together here and she went off in a huff. Then later she came back and said -you know I'm sorry I was a bitch."

"She did ?"

"Yes! She said, -just slap me next time."

"And did you?' Terry laughed.

"Ha ha ha ha. Can you just imagine that? Ha Ha Ah ha."

"Maybe she could slap Humpty Dumpty."

"Ah ha aha … oh, what then? She'd fall down!"

"Ah ha ha aha." Terry was laughing hard.

Terry and Jo just then got more silly. "We need more oxygen." The two girls lying on their backs on the rugged rock were laughing hysterically, "the air is too thin up here."

"We're in need of an oxygen rich environment like the NICU." They roared as lay under the open sky.

"Oh stop Humpty Dumpty you might fall and break your crown."

And they laughed until they had tears.

"Oh God Jo, I can just see us rock climbing we'd have to be separated."

"Yah or one of us would be dangling more than climbing." They took a minute to catch their breaths gulping air.

"Let's go eat," Terry said

And with that they drew in deep breaths, glanced around them at the other hikers and let out a few last laughs as they wiped their eyes now wondering how much they were overheard.

They hiked down the mountain talking about the date that Terry had and the new resident that was flirting with her.

At the bottom of the moutain, they stretched, talked with some people, and then went over to the café at the Biltmore for salads.

At the unit, the next day, of course, Jo's ring was the main talk at the scrub sink. "OH god it's beautiful," Lisa said.

"Did you see his mom yet, I mean did the family call you two?"

"Hey, my mother-in-law said, will that be one addition to the family or two? Like because his sister was pregnant when they got engaged."

"Joanna it's perfect," said Mary "I knew you two were going to get married now you can build your own family".

Good Bye

*T*hree weeks later Joanna called Sara's house to talk. She had seen Katie just two days ago. They had played in the yard with Dancer and then taken a walk about the neighborhood to where the swings were at the park. They sat on the swings together talking about how much fun they had together, how beautiful the sky was, and how new places held new adventures. That was the last time she saw her. "Katie?"

"Hi."

"Hi."

"Are you packed?"

"Yes. (Katie paused) Auntie Jo?"

"Yes, dear."

Michigan is really far away."

"Yes that is right, and you get to go on the airplane, that will be exciting."

"Aunt Sara says that it's a long, long way. I saw it on the map." Looking down she stood still for a moment and then said, "I'm wearing new sandals. I have new sandals."

"Yes, you do..." Joanna continued with Katie's shift in the conversation. "...and hiking boots for exploring and playing out in the snow. I will send you some letters and pictures, pictures of Dancer."

"OK, And I can visit you anytime I want to?" Katie said, repeating what she had heard before.

"When you're not in school or playing with your new friends and family. Bye, bye, sweetie you have fun," Joanna said wanting to keep the conversation light.

"Bye Jo Jo," Katie replied.

Joanna could hear Sara in the background calling. "Katie we have to go now."

"Bye, now," Joanna said one more time, and with that Katie hung up. Joanna held on until there was a dial tone. As quickly as the little girl came into her life, she was gone.

Joanna sat back on her sofa sinking into its plushy softness and thought about the opportunities life brought. One never knows when you would find yourself holding on tight to the present and when you would have to stand back and let go.

Opportunity is all around, Jo thought. Sometimes you give everything and what you hope to come from of it never happens, like adopting Katie. Sometimes, like with Brad, holding on had been the right thing to do. Now she would be happy with what she had. Katie was but a dream she dreamed, a vision. Joanna had this knowing that their time together was well spent. Sara said, "You'll find another girl," but Jo wondered.

L.A.

*I*n her bright red shorts and her navy sneakers with white laces, Joanna pattered about the deck overlooking the green hills and many houses of Malibu. She had accepted a travel assignment at St Peters hospital and they bought a townhouse on the edge of an exclusive neighborhood in Malibu, California just outside of L.A. They had sold their homes and Brad had help from his company with a relocation bonus and an inside housing tip. "Joanna, we don't need a big backyard. The ocean is our backyard," Brad said. And she agreed.

The sun shone brightly this late afternoon, just as bright as it did in Arizona. It was now the end of October. Malibu was all about great weather and they had enjoyed moving in September. It was close enough to the L.A. office but far enough away from the cramped city. Unlike Arizona, California was moist and Joanna could smell the fresh ocean air. Settling into a lounger, she read The Coast, a small weekly paper outlining the upcoming events. Reviewing the restaurant guide she picked out some lunch spots for herself and Dancer. Being new in town she had only a few girlfriends from work to be with on her days off from the hospital so she went out on her own sometimes taking her dog. The travel nurse company had turned out to be a great deal also paying her a monthly allowance for housing. She worked 12-hour shifts at the hospital three days a week with every other weekend figured in. Brad went into his office in L.A. every day. Some days Brad stayed late, and as Joanna's shifts ended late, when they did have an early dinner together it was special. Joanna was meeting new people all the time and there were a million things to do and see.

Reluctantly Joanna had sold her house and said goodbye to her neighbors and friends. Sara had thrown a great big party. The children, all a few years older than when they had first met, ran about with Frisbees and soccer balls, and Dancer, of course, chasing after them. It had been Joanna's first home of her own. The neighborhood had changed so much in the last year she lived there. Abigail, her one friend, who was not a mom moved across town. The Claybornes next door had divorced, and so did Bill and Sally several houses down. Pat and Michael had their first child and moved back east to their hometown. Mary Kelly was still home in her studio and Sara was always at a soccer game, a girl scout meeting or a PTA meeting. Life changes Joanna admitted and it was time for her to grow.

Although she did not have complete marriage plans with a ceremonial date, she had the company of the man she loved and was wearing a diamond engagement ring. Mary Kelly had said, "a diamond, is a diamond, is a diamond." Mary Kelly said that in her younger days she and Manny lived together until Mary Kelly found out she was expecting. "We just wanted to be together and we let things fall into place." Sara and Kevin had never lived together before they got married. It all didn't matter to Joanna anymore. They had thought about an Arizona wedding in the coming Spring, or maybe a small wedding in California after they settled in.

She told her friends, "When you love someone you have to see their side, their weaknesses and be willing to give them what they need." In this case, Brad needed time.

This week, Joanna had worked the last three days Saturday through Monday and now she had three off. Joanna loved the ocean and went several times a week to walk by the water, explore the shops or bike on the boardwalk. She was also discovering the city and the stores and restaurants there. "The Tradewinds Café," she read out loud. "It says fresh calamari deep fried, Cesar salads, and outdoor seating. Dance sounds like you can come too. Maybe tomorrow. What are we having for dinner tonight?" She put down the paper and leaned over the patio railing taking the view. As luck would have it, although it was her day off Brad was staying the night in San Fran, as she had come to call it. He had been called to work in the sister office and to attend a dinner meeting so he would also spend the night there. Jo padded into the kitchen, rummaged through the refrigerator and pulled out a neat package of hamburgers. She also placed on the granite counter some tomatoes spinach onion and some seasonings. On her upper-level deck, the barbecue was a shiny stainless steel built right in. Joanna flipped the button, waited a few minutes and then opened the lid placing her beef pattie on the sizzling grill. Remembering that there was asparagus in the frig. she went back to the kitchen to look for her vegetable grilling utensil. When she found it she went about preparing the asparagus for the grill. She sat at the patio table and enjoyed her dinner with Dancer looking on, as usual, hoping for just one bite.

Later she went downstairs with Dancer to walk her. Dancer had a red collar and today they looked really cute side by side Jo in red, white and blue and Dancer in red. As usual, some guys on the beach flirted with her. "Always the guys Dance." She commented. In the morning, Joanna got up early and ran 3 miles. At lunch time she drove to the restaurant she had picked out the day before, she in the front seat and Dancer in the back. She drove by a yoga studio and stopped to check it out. The girl there seemed really nice the floors were shiny wood, the front lobby area had yoga clothes and jewelry. She bought a bracelet and took a brochure.

"You can have the first class free so be sure to come by when you have time." The girl at the desk said. After lunch, she drove back and took care of some things at home.

When Brad came home he was tired and just wanted to watch TV so Joanna made the spaghetti while Brad made the garlic bread. "It's all about the seasonings," he said while buttering the loaf and sprinkling it with garlic and basil before placing it in the oven to toast. In the kitchen, they clinked their glasses of cabernet and kissed lightly. Soon the aroma of fresh Italian bread filled the townhouse and they settled down in front of the TV on their leather sofa, with the bottle of cabernet and homemade pasta.

That weekend they went out with a couple from Brad's work and Sunday they shopped together. This became their routine on weekends when Joanna was not working. They would go to the gym on Saturday morning, out to dinner Saturday night and on Sundays, they would do some shopping and things around the house. In the evening, Brad would start getting his papers ready for the week. Unlike Joanna, he kept his desk impeccably neat as he did his suitcase and clothes as if this is what mattered so much in life. Most every Sunday they would take a walk on the beach together. It was comfortable and easy. Some weeks Brad had to go to San Francisco for a day or two. It seemed that office was struggling as the accountant was found to be smuggling funds and the books were a mess. Besides legal work they needed someone of Brad's experience to continue the new work at hand while also dealing with the old records and figures. Brad's career began to take over his days, his evenings and some weekends.

The anniversary of her parent's passing had been eased this year by her new-found security in living with Brad in their California house by the beach. She sat out on the deck one day and conversed to her mom and dad talking to the heavens. She recalled how she and Brad had enjoyed celebrating by the ocean, the anniversary of their first date earlier in the month, going to Sea World and walking the entire grounds. After getting soaked from watching the whales they arrived at the dolphin pools to swim with the dolphins. They dawned wetsuits and listened to instructions. Then in groups of four, they eased into the pool and were assigned a dolphin. Brad and Joanna laughed at the dolphins chirping and silly antics and even held on to their fins as they raced across the water skimming and dipping.

They booked one night at the Ritz, so after the day at SeaWorld, they went to check in and dress for dinner. As Brad opened the door he scooped Joanna up and carried her across the room. "Honey, happy anniversary." He tossed her onto the bed and they bounced into each other's arms giggled a bit and soon lay face to face. "That was incredible Brad said, those guys are so smart you wouldn't think a fish, a big fish could be so smart. I like how they feel too."

"And you, you really went for a ride."

"I was so really holding on," he replied.

"Oh it was great Brad, I have always wanted to do that and it was amazing, even more, amazing than I thought it would be. I wish I had become a marine biologist."

"A biologist?" Brad repeated now pulling each of their bags up into the luggage stand.

"Yeah"

"Well, I guess it goes along with your geology stuff."

"I guess I would have been a veterinarian if I wasn't allergic to cats and well if I had been by the ocean, a marine biologist. You know my shells that I have. I used to have thousands more and I had labeled them all to genus and species when I was about 12. My grandma would send them to me and my mom and dad and I would go to Texas in the summer and collect them." Now undressing, she called out, "I got the shower first." And she disappeared into the shiny marble and travertine tiled bathroom leaving her clothes in a pile on the floor.

As they walked through seaport village in the coolness of the evening, Jo took Brads arm. There were many art galleries, dress shops, and curio shops. Wandering amongst the wooden buildings they talked and laughed. Joanna tugged at Brad's arm to take her to each and every gallery. In one shop the work of a new artist caught Joanna's eye. The work was an acrylic glass medium that seemed to have more than 3 dimensions as the lovers shaped within the luminous glass could be seen from many different angles ever changing their relationship to one another. A short while later they walked out having bought one of his glass sculptures for their home. It was so large they arranged to have it shipped to their home. For dinner, they ate Halibut, Crab legs, and escargot at a table that looked over the ocean. The moonlight shimmered across the lawns and garden as they strolled back to the hotel. Later in their high rise room, they snuggled in down pillows and made love with the sound of the ocean's waves still echoing in their minds.

The Neighborhood

As time went by they met more of the neighbors and people in their neighborhood and town of Malibu. In December, Joanna was invited by Linda who she had met at the mailboxes one day to attend a party given by her brother's friend who lived on Canyon Cliff Drive also in the neighborhood. As Brad was out of town this night it was good for her to spend some time with Linda. She met Linda at the party and they talked for about an hour while standing in the kitchen of the three million-dollar home crowded with all kinds of folks. Joanna and Linda talked about work, boyfriends and schools. They talked about Linda's plan to go back to Notre Dame to get her graduate degree. Lizzy gave her a tour of the house. Joanna especially adored the library with its mahogany bookshelves and unique artwork. They girls decided to start a book club and recruited Barbara to be a member before she left with congressman Tom Alley. Joanna laughed to herself "Tom Alley," thinking he looks like an alley cat if a person could so. There were all kinds of people at the party, all so different and when she asked someone where they lived they would say district 7 or district 6. Joanna had no idea which district she lived in. The language was quite different than what she used at work "the appropriations committee had set out ..., it was a non-partisan..., I'm never home I'm at the senate all day..., this week was rough one at the legislature". As it was getting late Joanna said her goodbyes and left.

She walked home down the few streets that separated the houses from the condos. She was feeling particularly good tonight despite reminding herself that she was going home to a house without a yard and would have to go back out to walk her dog who had been inside all night .... Such a trying week, she thought, no, month. December had been difficult as even with Holiday parties, Brad was gone to the San Francisco office more than she cared to have him go. Here she was on her own this weekend again. Now wondering if a promise was enough she walked through the gate. Why ever did she leave Arizona? She knew better didn't she?

At the condo she got the leash and then realized she left her homemade brownie at the party. Lizzy had made these awesome brownies and not being able to eat anymore she had accepted one Liz wrapped up for her to take home. What the heck she thought, now wearing jeans with her silk sweater. She zipped her leather jacket over her and went right back to the party with Dancer. "Say, hi again." She smiled her way right back into the kitchen to find the note with Barbara's number for the book club and her brownie all wrapped up as she had left them. "Joanna ! Hey, I'm glad you're back. Who is this cutie?"

"This is Dancer."

"She is so sweet. Say, Linda is going to pick the book and Valerie wants to join us. Oh, have you met Steve he lives next me at our place at The Cliffs"? Joanna and Steve and Valerie exchanged hellos and chatted a moment. "We will each invite a friend so to start our club and that would be eight!" Valerie was saying.

"This is great," Linda added.

"Well, I'm on my way back now nice to meet you again Steve and Valerie nice to meet you I look forward to the book club, besides I don't think Dancer was on the guest list." Jo said.

"Ah who notices? And she's such a good girl," Linda cooed as she bent down and scratched Dancer's ears

"Joanna wait I'll walk you back." It was Steve. "I'm not into the late, late show."

Joanna replied, "Hey Sure."

They walked out the high front door under the archway and down the drive through the spiked iron gates "I adore the lions heads. I guess anything animals I like."

"Well, I can imagine that comes easy when you have a dog like her. I always see you going out the gateway to the beach at The Cliffs."

"We love the beach, I'm from Arizona you know."

"Yes, you said that."

"It's a beautiful place but it was time for a change. I mean everyone was married with a million kids, you know? I do like the suburbs and having land around me. I used to give talks at the botanical gardens.

"Really?"

"Just an informal group gathering."

"No, really, to the botanical gardens."

"Oh, it's nothing like here. I love the plants here in California. My mom used to say I missed my calling. I had tons of plants in college -terrariums and all."

"I ah, have a spider plant and that's about it."

"Well, this is the place to have plants."

"I like to go to the aquariums around here Joanna if you haven't been to Birch's you really would like that," Steve told her about the tours and the research and more. They walked by the light of the moon the short distance down Wayfarer and on to Ridgeway parting just inside the entrance to The Cliffs.

"Thank you, Steve."

"Any time Joann."

Brad's family thought about coming to visit for the holidays but with everyone so scattered about the US, they all decided to wait until spring or summer to get together perhaps for the wedding. By late December, more often Brad was watching TV as if the conversation was too much effort. Saturdays he was in the garage with his cars and Joanna went to yoga class. He was preoccupied at the least or distant at best not offering his affection freely. Life as a couple was probably still new for him she thought. While she had almost always had a boyfriend, he had been solo most of his 35 years. He was sleeping on his side of the bed she noticed. He always fell asleep like a bear hitting the bed but something was bothering him. They were going on an outdoor weekend trip next week. It was to be a mini holiday vacation to explore more of California. Joanna hoped that being in nature among the trees, Brad would be himself again, his carefree self.

The drive was relaxing as they listened to the radio. She thought about telling him this weekend that she was 2 weeks late but then she had been late before. Although Joanna was hopeful she was also concerned, as they had agreed to wait before starting their family. If she truly was expecting a baby she wanted this to be a happy time, a right time for both of them, for all of them. So she thought to wait and see how things went and hoped his mood would be better.

At the lake, they hiked over some rolling hills and strolled the meadows admiring trees and what remained of the beautiful fall leaves. Inhaling deeply they enjoyed the fresh earthy air and also remarked how nice it was to be wearing jackets and boots. Brad remarked how Dancer's curiosity and sense of play perked up in the out of doors. The two were bonded as if he had been Dancer's owner all along. He threw sticks which Dancer ran after and carried for a distance before she dropped them in favor a scent she picked up, then squeezing underbrush and following wherever her nose led her. After a hike, they sat on the bench outside the cabin admiring the view.

The cabin had a big front door of knotty wood but it was also carved with great detail. Jo stood and traced over the carvings with her fingers. They went inside where leather and plaid furniture sat before a fireplace. They emptied their pockets of the leaves and rocks and such they had picked up onto the wooden coffee table. They took off their winter boots and had a soda before they went to the little town for burgers and milkshakes.

Holiday decorations greeted them and adorned the shops and restaurants. It was a quaint vacation type atmosphere and they talked to folks from other parts of California. After eating apple pie for desert they had pictures of themselves taken at the table. The coolness of the season was refreshing.

In the morning, they donned parkas and went boating and Dancer took to the boat just fine. She liked the bow. Her ears flopped in the wind when they went fast. They fished with some poles from the cabin and caught 5 trout, which they cooked for dinner along with oven baked potatoes, green beans, and salad. Eating dinner by the fireplace seemed like a cozy idea, so they took their plates and glasses over to the end tables next to the couch. After eating the apple pie and ice cream they had bought at the country store, they gazed into the colorful flames and the light from the fire reflected red and golden on their faces.

Brad found a deck of cards in the drawer and they played cards the rest of the night sitting on the rug before the crackling fire. It was a great weekend, new, light and relaxing. They never got into talking about marriage, the wedding, work, future plans or having children and that was OK, until the ride home.

As they drove home the next day, Joanna was what you might call bombarded by callings from what she thought was the world gone crazy. They drove past a giant billboard advertising a wedding chapel and then the chapel itself. Down the road, there was another advertisement for a baby store Babies R US. Then while stopping for sodas at the country store there was a father at the counter surrounded by two little ones chatting and touching the candy and cards and such that surround a counter and fascinate children. He was holding another smaller child and as he reached for his change the child squirmed out of his arms just as Joanna had come up behind and she caught him. Together this stranger and Joanna replaced the little boy safely in his arms. "Children fall for me," Joanna laughed, patting the little boy on his back. "Your OK," she said sweetly.

"Thank you, miss. He can be a handful. Come along Molly and Jeremy."

"I see," Joanna smiled looking back at the man and his family. He was only a few years older than Brad. She and Brad bought their munchies, some chips an apple and peanuts and got back into the car.

As they drove Joanna, thinking about her possible pregnancy, began to put her words together. But it was Brad who spoke first. "I am going to need to move for a while." Joanna's eyes grew big. "I need to be closer to the San Francisco office and I thought well.... I'd get an apartment."

"An Apartment!" Joanna exclaimed "No. We just moved what do you mean?"

"I know. "

"I have a contract with the hospital."

"I mean me."

"You?"

"Well just me."

"Just you Brad. Whatever you do... you're not serious."

"I need to. You can come up on some weekends."

"Weekends?"

"To visit"

"What about our house? You can come home."

Joanna became speechless. Somewhere between the wedding billboard, the joyous children at the store and her own little belly secret crashed this thunderous announcement of his. Her fear of abandonment began to surface and she became wild with anger. "You expect me to live by myself? I have put allot into moving out here for you."

"I have too, it's my job."

"Your job is in L.A."

"Well, I guess that was premature now that this San Francisco office is a mess."

"You're not the only one who works there."

"But this is the way it works."

"It doesn't work, not for me, I work some weekends and this is our house, and it just .... I don't want to live in an apartment. We need to be settled and to have space for us for our family."

"I have thought allot about it. I thought maybe we ...you would come with me but I'll be working ten hours a day, I need to get settled and figure this thing out."

"Figure out what?"

"Joanna I have been with this company for years I can't just say no."

"Why not? Why? You already moved once for them and I just got used to it."

"Let's just see how this works for awhile and then we'll take it from there."

"I'm not that type. I'm not international couple material. I want a family for gods sake. Next month I'm 31 do you want to wait until I'm 35 how about

40?" Joanna was pissed.

"I know." he said softly "I know you want more I just, right now,... I have to do this Jo. I don't feel like I have time for a family right now."

"But sometimes you just have to make the time."

"Did we have a great weekend or what Jo? This is quality time and we will do this again we don't have to be together every minute."

"That's not what I mean."

"We can still keep the beach house."

"Well yeah," she said flippantly."I'm living there. Then there was silence.

It was Joanna who spoke first, this time, more softly. "Dancer loves it and do you really have to work all weekend?"

"Look Jo sometimes I just need some space sometimes to just be me to get things done."

"I'm not following that thought at all."

"Well, it's enough pressure to be there, to take this opportunity...you ... well you need to be... Jo just give it a chance." Brad had little to argue with. He was consumed with his promotion with being a company man fixing the problems and rising to the top. Joanna was always supportive and fun and as well, she was very smart and he enjoyed her. Maybe someday they would have a family but that was not something he was ready for just now.

So the outdoor weekend folded. Over the Christmas Holiday, things seemed to go back to normal. It was a weekend of an annual church attendance, exchanging gifts, turkey dinner and phone calls to friends and family back home. Their house was brightly decorated with fresh pine tree, wreaths, and lights all around the patio's wooden railings. Evenings were special and they would walk the neighborhood most nights with Dancer before bed just to see the reindeer and snowmen and angel decorations.

The second week in January, after Joanna's birthday on a Monday morning Brad had several of his things together and was well packed for his new venture. Joanna stood there with Dancer on a leash. He came to her "Bye Joanna Oh Jo...", so sweetly he spoke as he gave her hug but Joanna was cool.

"We have to go." She announced. "We have an appointment," she said as she walked out the door first. She jumped in her car with her dog and drove off. "He actually did pack and leave and think I should be all kissy goodbye, I hate him." She said in her breath and to Dancer, "I don't need this I don't need him or anyone." And looking at Dancer she said with confirmation "Do we? We don't need anyone?" And a tear ran down her cheek. She drove the parkway along to highway one all along the beach and when she got tired they got out and walked. They were supposed to go to the vet but all of a sudden it didn't matter if they were a few minutes late. They sat on the beach, 'woman and her dog,' she thought. I don't need him I'll have my little girl and we will be everything for her right Dance? She watched the waves for hours sitting on a towel she had found in her car. She shivered until the sun began shining in between the scattered clouds. A few people walked by but mostly the beach was quiet. Calming down she thought how sharp she had been with him.

People have worse times than this. If he had not been acting so distant she would have told him. It was as if he was guilty, guilty of something. She wondered if they could still be close when they were together and what temporary really meant.

He phoned in the next day and Joanna let it ring. She heard his message but she wanted him to know, know that she didn't appreciate his springing this on her and being distant and all. Two days went by and she was again speaking to him. She missed him dearly. Why should she be the one in the back seat, last place, was she not smart, kind, pretty faithful? "For Christ's sake hire someone," she said.

"It's not that easy."

"When are you coming home?"

"I was thinking about next Saturday?"

It was Thursday "OK well will you call me this weekend? I don't like sleeping alone."

"I will."

"I have to go," she said wanting to close the conversation first. I have things to do, Dancer says Hi."

Unexpected News

"*I*t was, how does that saying go?" she said to Mary Kelly on the phone "What you think changes really stays the same. It's the same thing he's unavailable. I move all the fuck out here and he's unavailable." Joanna never swore. So Mary Kelly knew Jo was really upset.

But it caught her off guard and she gasped and laughed.

Trying to stay neutral and yet look out for her friend she replied, "You can never tell Joanna what life is going to bring you. Sometimes good things come from bad events and sometimes what we thought was bad, we look back years later and...."

"Mary Kelly, I'm pregnant."

Silence was the only response, and then...

"Oh my God."

"I'm 4 weeks late."

"Did you get a test?"

181

"I'm going to, just with the Holiday and Brad's new announcement...."

"Well, then you will have his baby Joanna. It is time and it will all work out. You have friends there don't you? or come home, just come home back to Arizona."

"I can't do anything now I just don't know."

"Well doesn't the baby change his plans a bit?"

"He doesn't know."

"Doesn't know? What are you thinking?"

"I don't want to use this little child to make things happen. He either loves me or not, he wants to be together or not, his family is first or his career."

"But Joanna he should know."

"He should know that people are more important than making money. I know he wants to get ahead and you know he's a little afraid of commitment that I thought that would change Mary Kelly I thought that we were so good together, but it's all about him again. He says he needs space."

"He said that?" Mary Kelly just listened. There is a time when friends just need someone to listen to them, just like when we talk to God. God listens, just listens and so that's what Mary Kelly did, just listen. Sometimes it takes an artist with a certain sensitivity to know that.

It was during the next week, feeling a little off Joanna slept late. Then it happened the pain and sickness. This morning found her retching in her bathroom. She went back in bed and her stomach ached and she thought being pregnant for sure was making her sick. She talked to her belly "little one everything will work out. You're very loved and long waited for." Having checked the calendar she had calculated that she was actually 8 weeks along. Being a nurse she didn't worry. Joanna usually ate healthy, took vitamins, and had been choosing water rather than wine. Next week she had an appointment with a doctor to confirm the home pregnancy tests she had done two days ago, but nature had its own schedule. In a few hours, she was very sick and she lost what would've grown to be the child she always wanted. She called Maylee, her nurse friend from work who insisted she go to the doctor now. "You're a nurse for gods sake."

"Exactly, and nature has taken its course. If I go in they'll just say I lost it and send me home with some pain pills. I don't want to sit around some office feeling awful and have people poke at me and tell me what I already know."

"You're impossible I'm coming over."

The two women went to see the doctor who confirmed what Jo had feared and expected.

Back home, Maylee tucked Joanna into bed at her beach home. She brought her tea and set out magazines she found in the family room. She thoughtfully picked through the magazines placing the ones with mother and baby articles on the bottom shelf of the bookcase. They sat together in

Joanna's room and Maylee offered conversation about the weather, the unit, the neighborhood, and the dog. She then read magazines in the living room by herself until she found Joanna had fallen asleep and then she went to sleep in the guest room.

When Joanna awoke she walked into the living room where Maylee was sitting on the couch. "You up? How are you?"

"You didn't have to stay overnight."

"Oh, Jo I didn't want to leave you."

"That was so sweet, you really didn't have to."

"Oh, I was too lazy to drive home that's all."

"I bet," Joanna smiled. It was nice to feel loved, to feel like she could not be good or well, and it was OK. "Thank you."

"Here let me make you something. How about breakfast on the patio."

The girls met the sun already rising midway in the sky. The wind gently blowing across the deck rippled the patio umbrella. January was a beautiful month, cool and crisp, but then nearly every day by the ocean was beautiful.

The week passed and Saturday came, Brad arrived home just before noon. Having left work behind, his attention was to Joanna. In their sweatshirts and jeans, they strolled a short ways on the beach to a spot and then settled in the sand to sit on a blanket. It was like they had just moved in. Brad seemed more relaxed. Joanna told him about the baby and the miscarriage and felt comfortable telling him. It was his reaction that she did not expect. "You should have told me, Jo. I am so glad your friends were here. I could have called my mother for you."

"That's sweet but I'd want you Brad not your mom."

"Oh, I wouldn't know what to do."

"It's just being there that's all."

"Well, I'm not actually ready for kids."

"Brad I'm a pediatric nurse, you have to know I want kids. Now I'm worried. What if we wait and I can't have them? I want to start planning our wedding and be able to be ready next time it happens."

"Um." Brad was quiet for a moment. "It seems so soon."

"Soon?"

"Oh, Jo I missed you so, Let's just be us this weekend." Brad put his arm around her and they sat close together on the sand she in his arms. "I'm sorry I wasn't here babe."

Monday came and Brad rose at 4 am to drive back to San Fran so he could be at work early. As he drove he felt splintered. He wanted to be with Joanna but his work was so important. He finally was exactly where he wanted to be. It was a no choice situation. He had worked and gone to college for this. Children he liked but now is not the time, maybe in a few years that would be about a right time for him. The sun had risen and he was close to his office now. He pulled into the garage and took the elevator up to his office.

The office was buzzing Monday morning. Brad and David met and took off for the deposition. David thought it was necessary that they be present, close by during the procedure. It took up their morning and part of the afternoon. Brad worked the rest of the day in his office to 6:30. On the way home he'd pick up Chinese food, stop for a burger or order pizza for delivery as usual. He was quite comfortable on his own after having lived solo all those years in Arizona. He called Jo just to say hi as he had forgotten to earlier. They talked a bit and said good night. This became the routine. Some weekends he stayed in San Francisco just watching a game on TV, going to the gym or doing some shopping. Driving or flying to Malibu every weekend was too much for the time they would have together. Joanna was not happy about the arrangement. She saw her future disappearing, and she began to realize that even if you love someone, sometimes you just don't want the same things. She studied yoga and meditation, went to her book club as well as nightclubs with friends. Valerie and Linda were always ready to go out for lunch or join her at yoga class. Some days, Maylee and Joanna shopped and some days Joanna would join Maylee and her husband Ben, for dinner at Maylee's house.

Joanna decided It was time to talk seriously. One Saturday Joanna and Brad sat on the couch at their beach home. "It's like so sad Brad, I really have to make a choice here and I think everything I thought was right is not. I remember my neighbors who divorced over children, actually two of them. One couple, she wanted a baby and got pregnant and he was totally anti-children so he left. The other couple down the street he wanted children and she didn't. They got married and when he wanted to start a family she just was not into it at all. She grew up with four brothers and sisters and she was the oldest by years and babysat all the time. She is really sweet but she just didn't want children in her daily life. You know I always wanted two or three, at least one. I can't wait for you to think you might someday want to try to have a family, and even without that issue I can't sleep alone all the time. I like you around me, but if that's not what you want we really need to make the decision."

"The decision to...."

"Be together or break up."

"You know I want to be with you. I can't see moving you and you getting a new job because I'm not sure how long I'll be in San Fran."

"It's not just us, it's the having a family."

"I'm not ready."

"And you may never be."

"It's not like I think about it all the time like you do."

Joanna was quiet, she had made peace with what she knew she had to do. Living alone and without children was not an option. It just could not be. She felt strong about her decision and her response was just to acknowledge his words. "Not all the time."

"You know I really care about you."

"I love you too, I guess we will have to be friends, maybe just friends. It's going to be…. we will have to just make that decision."

Neither one was happy about the outcome, but they went to bed together and held each other and made love, holding on to what they knew was familiar and what they had thought was for sure. Brad even stayed Monday night leaving for work on Tuesday. But all his words could not persuade her to wait to get through the rough times. As the weeks went by it became easier to accept the new situation but harder to accept the inevitable end and one weekend late April, Brad came to pack up the rest of his things leaving Joanna the beach house for now. They had a few friends over on Saturday night, had drinks and snacks and broke the news. They held each other at night and made love, giving validation to the relationship they had so cherished. Joanna hoped he would come home one day and say he was ready to try to be a dad to have a family, but it never happened. "I'll miss you."

"Me too", Joanna said, "me too."

When he left late on that Sunday afternoon her heart was broken and it sank even deeper as the day went on. She went to her room and when she looked about the room they usually shared. It seemed even bigger now that it was empty of his things. The chair with his jacket and pants were gone, the dresser barren now revealed scratched wood. She had done well last evening chatting with friends, eating lightly, following conversation and later strolling down the walkway. Now with the door to their room closed it echoed "alone". I am alone, she said to herself, without. Not- I am free, not -I was right, no she thought, I have emptiness. She dressed in her pajamas the drawstring bow lay flat against her abdomen. Her hair sleek & her eyes clear as if nothing happened. Crawling into bed she sipped hot tea. Her future was empty she thought. She thought of him sitting alone with boring people. How is it he prefers them to her? Later he'd be in bed and fall asleep like a shoe dropping. She sat in bed staring, magazines lay around her. She wished for a smaller room, a smaller bed and missed how she used to lay on his left shoulder and put her hand on his heart. With her heart empty and her room empty, there was nothing to do but go on to the next task. Now sleep then dress, then work, it all meant so little. She stared at the magazines. Why no tears, for tears were all she had before. No tears, no she promised herself. She knew she'd never ever be the same. She'd never love, never trust, never work, never be the same ever again, nothing seemed to matter. None ever stays. It was quiet and she was alone. How could she have pushed him so far? How could he have pushed her? He had promised. It was the promise that changed everything, that ruined everything. It was the promise that became the promise that was never kept. There would be no spring wedding. Maybe he just wanted someone to go with him, someone to help him fit in and get settled in his new area then it was on to the next project. To succeed in a business venture was his all-consuming life. How could he not see that having success with no one to share it with was not really success at all?

Summer at the Beach

*T*here had been many days when Joanna did not want to get up. She wanted only to do nothing, just nothing. She took first cancel from the hospital whenever she could and a few times she called in sick. After pouting for a few weeks she felt better and calling in sick to work again today, she was going to make this a day of her own, a day of beauty to appreciate and enjoy the beauty of what was, not what was not. It was time for a new attitude. She gathered her duffle bag and some simple Keds to walk the beach, a scarf for her hair and Dancer's leash and dropped them at the door. Over her legs, she pulled on windbreaker beach pants that tied in the front. They were sail blue. Her t-shirt was white and yellow and she had a matching yellow and blue hoody which she tied around her waist. "Come on Dance," she said as she grabbed her Maui Jim's off the table and put them on. With Dancer's ears and tail in the air they made their way down the gravel and sand path to the beach.

The air that met them was fresh and misty. It smelled of salt and Joann loved this one thing that she could never have in Arizona. The waves at the beach were rolling and being a weekday there were not too many people on the sand. "Let's run, Dance." And off they went. Soon the Keds were off, her pants were rolled up, and Joanna was splashing at the water's edge while Dancer trotted beside her biting at the waves. They walked and walked and walked. They stopped for a juice drink at the beachside café. Joanna leaned against the counter with Dancer sitting in the shade. She never removed her glasses as her eyes, she feared they would say more than she wished to reveal. "Guys, eh I have no attraction to any of these guys." Some were young 20 something surfers, some were middle age hippies. She thought if that's what makes them happy, a life with very little money then they were doing the right thing. A few couples were vacationing and then always there were children and mothers running after them... The mothers would be with other mothers and sharing stories of their children's lessons. "Hello," she replied to someone at the counter. "Oh yes, lovely day. Thank you," she replied as she paid.

And they walked and walked from the sandy beach to the board walk's end, to the sandy beach, past parks and sculptures and shops and swings. She was just open enough to stop and pick up a sailing brochure

"You a sailor?"

"Always wanted too."

"It's not hard you know we take you or we teach you."

She looked behind the man to the billboard on the

wall that read: sailing cruises, sailing tours, and sailing lessons.

"Oh thanks, I'll think about it."

"OK, Miss you have a nice day."

There was something so nice so inviting about how he said have a nice day, something so simple that you hear all the time. He was an older guy, not pushy, it was like he enjoyed what he did and his energy was contagious.

She stuffed the brochure in her bag.

The sun now setting they turned about to walk as far the other direction. The walk home was long but it was good for her wearing her out enough that when she went to bed she actually slept well.

May was over, it had come and gone in what now seemed like a heartbeat, though living through it was like an eternity and though her unrest was still with her it lessened every day. Joanna rose and walked to the window looking out over the horizon into the blue sky. It was a Monday morning in June, she had a great weekend. Finally, she was released from the ties that entangled her to Brad, or so she had thought so Saturday night when she made love with Jay. She had met Jay at a beachside café while walking Dancer. He flirted with her and he was just nice to talk to. They had met several times during the last three weeks by chance and so this one day she sat with him on the beach and accepted his kisses. It was nice to be held to feel someone attracted to her. He told her how she had a good energy and how great she looked and she had corrected him saying that most of her shorts were too tight. "Hagen Das," she said. "Almost every night it's Hagen Das for two only there is only one person eating it for the last two months."

"How long were you together?"

"Three years, three years and I moved out here. I left my house, my house on the mountain," she said sadly. " I ah..." Joanna wiped her eye.

"Hey, you don't want to talk about that stuff ."

Joanna smiled "I ah ....

He turned his head closer and kissed her right there on the beach with everyone around and it didn't matter. He was probably too young for her but he was cute. She hadn't known him long and he was a painter, an artist who walked on the beach for inspiration. He taught art to children at the art school. Who cares anymore who is watching and how long I have known him and what he does for a living and how old he was. It didn't matter anymore. It had been months since Brad had moved into his new place. Brad was gone and it was time she moved on. Though she said it over and over she still felt somehow betrayed and tied to her past. This day Jay had awakened something in her and she decided she was going to let things happen. Their date was for the following Saturday.

There had been so many days when she did not even want to get up. She really wanted to do nothing just nothing. She took the first cancel whenever she could to be off work and a few times she called in sick. When Saturday came Joanna was actually excited. They were to go out for sushi and Japanese beer. Dressed in a strappy silk blue dress, sandals and some beaded stone jewelry she bought on the boardwalk, she went to meet him at the restaurant. Her long blonde hair which she usually wore straight and lose she had cut short just the day before. It now fell to meet the top of her shoulders in layers going every which way. She looked hip and she was enjoying the guys who noticed her as she walked from her car to the restaurant. Jay met her wearing jeans, leather sandals and a casual button up shirt in that wrinkled style. It was refreshing to see someone dress fun, unlike Brad who most always wore dress pants, ironed with a crease, and at his most casual he wore loafers. Joanna believed that successful people didn't have to always be dressed up in business wear. Brad thought otherwise. These thoughts took only a second. As Jay smiled she felt bright and happy. "Hey there."

"Hi, yourself," Joanna replied

"You look great" Jay replied standing by the aquarium of exotic fish.

Joanna tossed her head side to side to make her hair swing giggling, "Isn't it great?"

"Really nice" and he touched her hair

"Bluebell," Joanna was noticing the fish.

"Aren't they cool?" Jay said, "I love this place."

The hostess addressed Jay asking about seating

"Two." He replied and looked at Joanna. "At the sushi bar?"

"Oh yes, that's fun."

They ordered hamachi and sake and California rolls and Japanese beer. They talked about when they first met and things they had said and people and the children they frequently saw on the beach. Jay had a fun sense of humor and soon they were laughing.

After dinner, they walked about the streets that were filled with all different shops. They talked and laughed and Jay wanted to escort Joanna home. She replied lightly "OK."

At the door, Jo said, "You have to see my new house." She had told him how she had redecorated the whole place in the last few months it was all about new energy Joanna said. In the living room, they talked on the sofa and left a trail of clothes into the bedroom where they made love for hours until they fell asleep and then in the morning she awoke in his arms. They showered together in her bath and in the kitchen, he made eggs while she cut fruit and made protein smoothies. "Hey, what's this? Hagen Das in a protein drink?"

Joanna laughed "I promise next time I'll buy the ice milk."

They walked out to the deck and sat down. "What are you thinking Joann? Shall we make some art?" Jay said

Joanna smiled from her chaise looking across at him. "I don't know."

Smiling he replied, "Some art material my dear. What do you have we can play with?"

"I think there are some watercolors or pencils in the desk."

"What about some shells?"

"Oh sure, "Joanna laughed, "I have a ton."

They gathered some things together and soon were gluing the shells into a sculpture of seagulls. Totally immersed in the whole project the time went by fast. Jay added some details with paint. Joanna ran to another room to get a piece of driftwood for the base. After a few hours, they sat admiring their work. Later, at her front door, they kissed goodbye and she watched just for a second from the window as he walked away. Joanna placed the new artwork on her coffee table looked about then decided to put it higher on the bookcase.

Today she reflected on her new romance. Were her feelings the all in love kind or what were they? This was just for fun she reminded herself. Steve had been asking her out for weeks now. He lived around the corner in their community his deck facing South. Joanna would see him at the mailbox the pool and on occasion at the market. He had met Brad, but they had never been buddies. Brad was more into his work than he was his into friends. Steve knew that they had parted and never asked more about it.

There were other men asking her out. At work, few people knew that she has broken up with Brad. She had worn her diamond ring only occasionally to work but then many hospital nurses didn't wear their diamond rings at work. She admitted only that Brad was transferred to a new division and they were working on things. The nurses responded, "Get a new travel position." And a radiologist suggested they play tennis but she changed the subject dodging his offer as she didn't want her workplace involved in her personal life.

Joanna now had girlfriends who actually called her and looked forward to shopping or swimming with her. Sunday she drove to Maylee's house. Maylee also lived in Malibu. She was married to Ben who was a lawyer. Maylee had a swimming pool and invited Joanna and Dancer. She had no problem with letting Dancer swim in her pool, in fact, she encouraged it. "Go get the ball!" Dancer leaped thru the air splashing into the deep end retrieving the tennis ball, she swam to the steps and shook off. The girls clapped their hands from their sun chairs on the deck tossing the ball over and over. Soon they too were in the pool swimming and chatting and batting around a beach ball.

It had been a full weekend the fun faded into Monday and the week ahead. So the summer passed with fun times with Jay, book club meetings with Linda and Valerie and the girls, and swimming with Maylee. They were no longer distractions from her life, they were the people that made up her life, especially Maylee. Maylee and Joanna went to the mall together and shopped in the same clothing stores- it was everything BCBG, J Crew, Banana Republic and Lucy Lu's. They ate at the cafe's and walked on the beach Tuesdays or Saturdays and went to yoga class on Wednesday nights. Some nights Joanna joined Maylee and Ben for dinner and drinks and a game of scrabble.

About a Year Later

*I*t was the following April when Joanna decided it was high time to follow through on learning to sail. First, she decided to go and be the passenger for the day and to observe and learn about sailboats. Linda came to Joanna's house and the two went down to the marina and hopped on board for a day cruise. They had a great day sailing to Coronado Island and back. So Joanna signed up for her first sailing lesson.

The morning came when it was her lesson day. She was well prepared having already studied her manual. The sun streaming through her window seemed to be beckoning her. Perhaps it foreshadowed what the day would bring into her life. This was, for Joanna, just an idea an adventure, something to do because it was there. And well, she thought, you never know when you will move again to another place or city and the opportunity will be gone like so many other things.

Dressed in Keds for deck shoes, shorts and a tank she grabbed her cap from the closet by the door and a bag with a towel. Today she drove the few miles to the sailing school because it would be a long day. She arrived and waited until they boarded the sailboat. "I have another couple of people coming," Gilbert said. Soon they could see a group of people walking toward the boat. Gil helped her onboard before checking in two other students. Joanna walked the deck reviewing some terms and locating by name the winches, the boom, and life lines. "And the halyard is here," she said under her breath. As she looked up from her spot in the cockpit at the stern of the boat, she saw the two other guys walking on board. She tilted her Maui Jim sunglasses and looked again before lowering her glasses. "Oh my God!" The guys stepped toward her and Alex turned his head.

"Joanna?"

"Alex?"

"Wow, my gosh Joanna from Arizona …."

"You all know each other?" Gill interrupted.

Alex continued his gaze and was now smiling. "Joanna it is such a surprise, it is so nice to see you. This is my friend John."

"Nice to meet you."

"Well, that makes things easier. We're going to review some terms so when we are underway I can be sure you will know what I'm asking you to do." Gil said.

"Great, oh so are you on vacation?" Alex said to Jo.

"No, I live here."

"You do?"

"How about You?"

"Yeah I have place here just up...."

"You know each other from Arizona." John interrupted before he went over to help Gil pull some equipment from the storage compartments below.

"So how are your family and your wife?" Joanna asked.

"Oh, Jo we have been divorced a while now."

"Really I am so sorry, that is so sad."

"Oh, not really I am so much better for it, in the long run, it was just not meant to be. My parents are still in Scottsdale. But you, I thought, I heard you got married."

"Well no, ah almost, and so I am learning a new trade," she joked, holding up her sailing manual. "I always wanted to sail, it's so wild that you are here too. This will be fun."

They stepped off the boat onto the wooden dock where the 40- foot sailboat was tied, to prepare for sea. Its silver mast extended way up into the sky glistening in the sunlight. The ropes and pulleys that hung from it blew in the wind so as to clatter rhythmically against the metal. A few seagulls flew overhead and squawked as Gil reviewed sailing terms with his students. He first assigned Jacob to take the helm. While motoring out the channel Dan asked for the names and meanings of the various buoys.

After the traffic in the channel cleared of other boats, Katrina pulled up the jib sail and Joanna cranked the winch while Jacob at the tiller steered out to the ocean. Taking turns at steering the boat, coming about and jibing the boat the group became sailors in the wind and of the sea.

At the helm, Alex and Joanna took turns as did Katrina and Dan. They also had time to sit and visit and make new friendships. While sitting on the bow of the boat, Joanna and Alex dangled their feet in the ocean mist. The boat surfed the waves rocking up and down as the sail filled, and Dan back in the cockpit, steered high into the wind. They pulled up the large spinnaker sail that was all colors of blue and it filled full and round with the ocean's wind. It was here on the bow of the boat that Alex asked Joanna for a date and the two wondered if they should've been the one's to marry and that Brad and Shawn would've been perfect for each other. They laughed at the thought and found pleasure in making fun of their x- lovers. Joanna accepted his invitation and they decided to go for lunch that very next Friday.

Friday they walked the pier and stopped in the shops. Joanna bought a card and Alex bought a kite. They talked liked they had been best friends forever. Easily each of them touched upon their failed relationships. Shawna had had an affair leaving Alex and Alex had taken up golf and avoided dating. He was about done with his project in California and was planning to move back to Arizona. On the boardwalk, Alex unfolded the kite and set it free in the wind. As he ran she ran with him. He took her hand and with their faces toward the sky they watched the kite twirl and soar. The red and white paper ruffled with the wind. After a while, they collapsed in the sand not worrying about getting sand on everything. Sitting on the beach he replaced the kite into the bag and they went for lunch. It was a pleasant afternoon ending with a kiss at Joanna's beach house where Alex dropped her off. It was later that night when Alex called to see if Joanna would be free for dinner Sunday. Joanna had to work and he had a deadline to meet the coming week so he suggested they make it the next Saturday. Joanna accepted without hesitation.

This Saturday at Maylee's house, Jo and Maylee painted wooden bird houses for their patios. Joanna had bought them at a craft store. Joanna painted a cactus and a cockatoo on her bird house while Maylee painted musical notes and flowers on hers. "You know what would be great?" Joann asked, "…is to glue on some beads like really tiny beads, for my bird's eye and on your flower centers."

"Oh yeah, that would be good. Let's go up and look in the attic. I have some things up there and I have an old chair I want to show you. I was thinking about painting it for the patio. You could help me paint a design on it." Maylee continued, "I have a lot of things that were my grandmother's and my mother's. My mother thought we would use in our house. Ben and I just haven't had the time to get to everything.

The two women climbed up the attic stairs to a tiny space in which they had to hunch over and then sit to sort through the boxes. Maylee opened a jewelry box and Joanna opened an old novel. "This is a real antique necklace, and this one, I like this one. Isn't it sweet?" Maylee said to Jo handing her one of the necklaces. "I'd never wear it, though. Oh, this...this was my dad's. My first dad's," she clarified, as she handed the pin to Joanna. "He was in the service."

"Is this him?" Joanna remarked taking the photo she found from the book she held and handing it to Maylee.

"Yes, that's him! My dad was in the service, mom never married him. I mean mom loved him but it was a different time and he was married to someone else. She said it was a time when they were both lonely and they were there for each other. I never really knew my biological dad but my mom married someone else very shortly after." Jo looked sad for her. "It was all OK Jo. I love my parents and I always knew them as my parents even though my other dad was not here." For Maylee, never was there a time she could remember when her parents were not around for her.

"Look over here, see I have a few more of photos of them, but I look more like my mom."

She began to sort out and pull photos of her dad from a scrapbook.

"My dad was in the service too," Joanna said.

"Really Jo you never told me, I know that... well, I hope, ah. Joanna, I am sorry about that accident your parents had in Europe." Maylee placed a hand on Joanna's lap.

"Oh May it was so long ago, and you know they had a good life."

"This is him, this picture is better." The women with their heads together looked closely at the picture.

"Oh my gosh," Joanna called out. "He looks just like my dad. This is your dad?"

"Of course silly. My mom doesn't keep a picture of old air force men around for history's sake," she said, handing Joanna another photo. "They all look like that in uniforms. "

"But May," Jo exclaimed holding another picture, "This is my dad! OMG, my dad had a lover. Oh my God...." The two women's eyes grew large as they looked at each other rather blankly.

"Can not be Joanna. Let me see," Maylee replied taking the photo. "That's him that's my father." She searched for another photo scattering the old pictures around her. "Here is a better one."

Joanna took it and then gasped. In that moment, a tear began to trickle down her cheek.

She felt she couldn't even breath. She paused before she looked up and her eyes once again met Maylee's. The two woman just stared at the man in the photo.

Maylee broke the silence. "We're sisters Joann! Do you know we are sisters!"

"Sisters! Joanna exclaimed not caring about the affair, not sinking into her past but embracing her future. "Oh May," she cried. "Oh May," as tears welled up in her eyes.

Maylee wrapped her arms around her. Joanna did the same embracing her new found sister. " ...and we like the same things!" she declared while sniffing her tears, tears of joy.

"Joanna Styles, my friend, my sister what about that? Mom will just be ... oh what will she be? You know she adores you."

Forgetting about the beads for their project they made their way downstairs. The afternoon sun streaming through the clouds into the stain glassed window of Maylee's kitchen found the two women sipping lemonade and telling family stories while sitting at the table.

Their relationship had a new found meaning and it was for each of them a wonderful surprise.

Joanna was so excited she immediately called Sara when she got home. Sara did not answer so she dialed Mary Kelly.

"Oh my God Jo! You have a sister? Wow talk about chances and she is your friend right?"

"I know, I know we do everything together."

"I mean what are the chances?"

"She's about my size you know slender with dark hair and I think we have the same nose."

"You're getting the family you always wanted Jo. That means her mom is like your step mom?"

"I don't know the terms."

"Did you talk to her family yet?"

"No I just got home and we found out today."

"That's crazy. So when are you coming to Arizona we miss you around here?"

"I thought I'd come out in October when it's not so hot. When's your next show?"

"It will be around then or maybe November. I'm waiting for a creative flow you know some new inspiration. A sister, I still can't get over it."

"Me too. I wonder what Alex will say."

"Alex?"

Oh, Mary Kelly I met up with Alex my friend from the University. He was on the sailboat. I took a sailing lesson and it was all day. I have a sailing license now. I had to take a test and everything. It was fun, kinda hard especially the docking part."

"Well, you go girl."

"Oh, how are your girls?"

The ladies talked almost an hour catching up on every event they had missed out on in each others lives for the last few months.

That night Joanna took out her albums, her box of odd pictures and sorted through them. She held a photo Maylee had given her. She was filled with fond memories as she spent the night looking through her albums and her mom's and dad's albums, and boxes of family stuff that she had saved. Before bed, she rearranged the framed photos on her dresser and looked for a photo of herself and Maylee to add to her set. She was working the next two days in a row so she made it an early night. Settling into bed she felt content.

That week the NICU was busy as usual. There was the noise of many alarms, the activities of the new deliveries, the social workers, the respiratory therapists and of course new residents attending rounds. Always there was some ethical dilemma. A baby was born hooked on drugs to an alcoholic prostitute and the father was unknown. A baby was born with no brain, only a brain stem. She was perfect in every other way.

Another two babies were born, they were twins, and both were cute as could be. Their father owned a pizza store. Joanna affectionately called them the pizza twins. One was much larger than other. The dad came in and said, "he's my little sausage and he is my pepperoni." Joanna enjoyed her job and relished in the good news.

Saturday's date with Alex was better than a date, for each of them it was as much a reunion as it was a blossoming love affair. The had great conversation and a wonderful dinner. It was first of many dates and many nights they would spend together. They talked about Arizona and about their families. They talked about sports and sailing and their favorite movies. While driving home they made plans to go the concert on Friday. At her front door, Alex wrapped his arms around her and she returned his embrace pausing a moment recognizing that feeling that she had known so well or so she thought so but now she doubted herself. Stepping back, Joanna said good night. After saying good night. Alex walked to his car stopping to turn around and be sure she had safely closed her door. He hummed along to the radio as he drove home.

Friday's concert was to be performed by three of the American Idol singers and musicians. Alex arrived at 6:30. He waited by the door as Joanna gathered her things. Outside he opened the door to his SUV and after she settled in he closed it gently. While buckling himself in he welcomed her to adjust her seat and chose a CD or radio station. As they drove rather than old memories they talked about themselves now and how they became interested in sailing.

At the concert hall, Alex guided her in ahead of himself. In the aisle, an usher directed them to their seats. She sat on his left. They stood and cheered, they sang along and had a great time. Music, clapping and dancing filled their night. Being together was easy there was no pretense and no holding back. Alex took her home and they held hands as he walked her to her door. On they step they stood for a moment. As soon as the key turned it was as if a match lit on fire. They entwined their arms as their lips met hungrily for a greater closeness. Joann led him to her room. A trail of clothes lay behind them. On the bed, they made love and declared their passion that had been forever stirring burning in their hearts from years past.

In the morning as Alex dressed to leave he asked her to have dinner with him that night.

"Oh, that's sounds wonderful."

"You pick."

"Ok. Sushi," she replied.

At 7 he picked her up. She wore a teal blue silk top that made her blue eyes seem even bluer. It dipped slightly to reveal that smallest bit of cleavage of her full breasts.

Alex kissed her hello. His tall frame leaning over her. "Umm I adore you," he said with great pleasure and confidence. Joanna smiled in return admiring his broad shoulder and strong arms. She leaned in and returned his kisses and taking his hand she said: "let's go."

Tonight they walked to the sushi restaurant. It was a favorite of Jo's. They stopped to admire the fish aquarium before taking seats in a booth. In the restaurant, while they waited to be served, Alex folded a small paper over and over until he made a tiny bird. All the while she watched. He placed it in front of her. "Oh, how wonderful. show me how." Joanna exclaimed.

Alex made the first fold. Then he took her hands and placed them under his. Gently he turned the corners to the center and the side to the right and then the left and so on.

"Oh, we made one. Let's make three."

Dinner came and they shared various sushi rolls, noodles, and cucumber salad. There was something special about Alex. She felt it in looking into his eyes which seemed soft and honest, and his touch that was strong but gentle.

In the weeks and months to come, they went to movies and Alex joined Joanna at her yoga class. Partner yoga became a favorite date for them. They went shopping and out to dinner every week. Saturdays were for outdoors hiking or walking and sometimes they went sailing.

One day having lunch on the patio Alex asked Joanna, "Have you thought about moving back? I mean do you plan to stay in California?
"It's been an adventure, but I feel like Arizona is my home."

"I planned to move back. I think I was supposed to be here to meet you again, for us to meet again." He corrected himself. "Joann, before you say things, I know what you are saying and when you are calling me. I've dreamed of our future like a knowing. When I sit next to you in yoga I feel your depth. I know you're not just thinking about lunch." He reached over and poked her belly. He liked to tease her about how much she ate.

"It's my center, I have to feed it." They both laughed.

"I feel you too. I know before the phone rings that you're going to call. I like all the things we do together and I haven't even met your family.... I'm happy Alex I'm happy we are together." She moved over to his side of the bench. They watched each other, being together was easy. They planned to take a day trip in Alex's jeep the next weekend that she was off.

Saturday came and when Joanna heard the jeep pull up she ran downstairs. Standing in the doorway of her beach condo she watched him make his way up the drive. Seeing him her heart jumped, she knew he was the one. The morning sun behind him outlined his body. He was tall like Brad, creative like Jay, a family guy like Kevin, and a little like her dad. His career in architecture seemed to ground him she thought. He had all the qualities she had imagined and hoped for in a man, a husband. The man she had given up looking for.

The jeep was behind him, it was his fun car and they were going to cruise the washes or the dunes today. They were taking Dancer with them too. Dancer would be belted in the back with her harness. They had all been out in the jeep before with the roof-top open and the wind in their faces bumping up and down playing CDs and singing. She loved how he was with her.

Alex smiled and strutted across the drive as if he had a secret. One hand was swinging along in stride, the other was behind his back. He looked at Jo and looked and the ground alternating his glance before calling out "good morning."

"Hey, babe." As he approached she jumped down the few steps. He reached his arm out to encircle her waist pulling her toward him and kissing her. She returned his kissed and he stood back a step.

"Daisy Duke's and hiking boots, your so cute."

Joanna laughed. "Thank you, you're not so bad yourself."

He wore a light blue T-shirt from the Beach Hut with a white sailboat and logo on it pulled over gray cargo shorts. He brought his other arm out from being his back which he'd been holding back. His fist was clenched as he extended his arm.

"What is it, what do you have?"

"Well, you have to open it to see." With that, she unlocked his fingers one by one and he dangled a silver chain with pendant. It was a beautiful blue stone.

"It's a moonstone!" She said.

"It is. You are the sun and the moon to me, dear Joanna."

"Oh, let's put it on."

He reached his hands over her shoulders as she leaned into him. The morning air was cool on her neck as he fastened the silver chain. He stood back as she looked down holding the circular bezel and stone that fell just between her breasts.

"It's really pretty. Thank you."

"Your welcome. I love you," he whispered in her ear

with all the passion he felt. Her body warm, her arms cool, they hugged feeling that oneness, a peace they shared.

Dancer was now at their feet. She had snuck up on them. For once she was not begging for attention nor did she try to stand between them. Dancer sat on the step admiring the beautiful morning. Yawning loudly she arouses their attention and Joanna and Alex laughed.

"Hey, let's get going."

"Ok, let me get our lunch. I packed a little cooler." Minutes later they were off. It would be a day of wind and water, rocks and gravel, and sand and brush.

Cruising along the trails by the ocean they went from rough road to main roads by vegetable stands and countryside, by shell shops and restaurants. It was fun just to drive with no errands and no plans. They ended up finding a spot near the docks and sat down to eat. They were far north. A man came by and told them about the house he just bought. He'd just moved back to California after living in Nevada for years. Two girls in their twenties walked along as another boat pulled up in the distance. The girls jumped in and the boat took off. A guy standing on a paddle board was making his way thru the waters around the marina. He seemed to have perfect balance. "They're the new thing now," Jo said.

"I've seen a couple of them.... Hobbie's. People take them everywhere."

"I'd rather a boat. It looks like the water is too rough for that."

"Boating is the best for sure. We could try it some day though if you want, maybe on the lake."

"That sounds fun." They threw the extra bread out for the birds and walked about with Dancer.

Later at Joanna's they changed before going for dinner. At the table, Alex had a lot to say. "I was looking at the maps we had out the other day. There's a nice acre lot near your old neighborhood. There's a development nearby, some tract homes. I think an acre is all we need."

"Oh yes, that's perfect, enough for the house, kids, dogs, and a garden." Joanna glowed.

"Remember the blueprints I showed you at my office when I showed you the home I want to build someday. I want to build that with you."

It was no surprise to Joanna. When you know, you just know, she had thought. She smiled in response.

"What do you think about getting our place under construction? If we want we can finish the East wing first and live there while the rest is built or we can live in that resort you like."

"It sounds great. I'll get my job back and we can see Sara and Kevin and Mary Kelly and your family too."

"Unless you want to do something else."

"I think it would be fine."

"Well then miss Joanna we'd better get those drawings finished up with your input of course. Then I need a little drawing from you."

"From me?"

Pushing a napkin toward her he said, "What kind of ring do you like?"

It was that date that led to the night at the beach, the night that became forever special for both of them.

All the Elements Meet

On an August evening, Alex and Joanna sat on the beach watching the waves. "This is where all the elements of life meet, Earth wind and water," Joanna said. "I guess that's why I like it so much."

"And this...." Alex said, "is where I once again found you." He took her hand and said,

"You were always the one."

She smiled back at him needing nothing. "I love you." It was often that they said I love you to one another. His presence, his friendship, and his love were enough as were her dog and her career. Life was good and fun and peaceful.

"Marry me, Joann," Alex said.

"Marry me and I'll always be with you." In his words were the promise, nothing rehearsed, nothing long and dragged out.

Out of his pocket, he took a black box which he opened. Her smile widened as she looked into his eyes and he into hers.

"It's beautiful." There was no questioning. Waves breaking onto the shore and hitting rocks threw mist into the air. She leaned into him, as she was already tucked as she was under his left shoulder, her hand reached out with her fingers splayed open to receive the ring. As he placed the ring on her finger the sky sparked a glowing star and the diamond sparkled in return. They wrapped their arms around each other as their lips met in the kiss, the kiss of all time, their past their present and their future.

By November, Alex was now staying at Joanna's quite frequently. His condo suite, which the company paid for, which had become a place for pit stops, forgetting things and leaving things now held only a few boxes. They had set their wedding date for December fifth. It would be a Christmas wedding with black and white suits and dresses and red roses and red bride's maid dresses. Maylee was to be her maid of honor and the two vowed to visit one another and share their families long into the future. At Joanna's house, Alex's stuff was mixed in with her stuff and neither of them were too particular other than hanging up silk shirts and nice clothes. Their sandals they tossed in a pile by the front door. His architecture digest magazines were mixed with her novels on the end tables but over in the corner he had a desk of his own which they had purchased at an antique sale.

After a run on the beach late this afternoon, Joanna came in and ran up the stairs.

"Hey, Babe how was your run?" He looked up from his desk. "Your soo wet isn't the water freezing?"

"Had to run in the water, just had too." Joanna's

crop pants were wet and her lips were blue. "Talk to you in a minute," She said, as she ran into the bath.

"OK."

She ran the water to get it hot, dropping her clothes to the bathroom floor, she looked in the mirror at her breasts full and round, her abdomen smooth and slender, her legs long. She was still lean and good looking though well aware of years. Soon she would be 33. Thoughts of having babies always touched her mind yet she didn't want to worry about it. It was too big of a world of what ifs and in time, well, it would happen. There was hope with this body. She worked hard to keep it strong and healthy.

As she was leaning into the mirror her left hand sparkling with the diamond from Alex, he appeared at the doorway. "Oh," She called out startled by his presence.

"Say are you..." he was taking off his T-shirt over his head and baring his muscular chest. "Do you want company, honey?" He said lovingly. He stood next to her looking at her through their reflections in the mirror. "You're in great shape."

She smiled. "and look at you!" And they admired their reflections.

"We make a great couple," Alex said. " You were always the one Joanna I'm so glad we are together now."

His chest and arms were strong and his eyes a deep

brown and his hair windblown and curly. He picked her up and turned about placing her back where she had stood. He placed his hand flat on her stomach and moved around behind her to embrace her with both arms.

Still talking to each other's reflections they exchanged words of love and smiled while their eyes sparkled. He breathed in with his face in her soft long blonde hair that fell about her shoulders and kissed her ear. "Your hair always smells so good."

"Alex?" she said shortly, pretending she was annoyed.

He smiled, "Honey your soo beautiful."

She smiled leaning back into him.

And with their clothes off now and with him standing with her she moved to him and he to her. They rocked in a slow dance with his hand still around her waist and the other about her hips. She stroked his arm with one hand and sighed in delight. He was so warm and wonderful. She felt his strength as she arched her back and sighed in delight. Her sounds turning to gentle laughs of pleasure and then he joined with her in his breath and pleasure. Holding her close he said, "my love, Joanna, my love..." and with humor, he added, "run away with me now to the waterfalls of the endangered rainforest." She laughed and smiled and they twirled about stepping into the shower.

In two days they were moving back to Arizona where they were having their wedding at the church that Alex had attended as a child. They were planning a family too as soon as possible after that. Their new house they were having built on the mountain. The property across Dixeleta Road, that Joanna used to pass on her running path was being built up into subdivisions and plots of land were for sale. They were not small lots either. They were huge and with their two incomes and the sale of the Malibu place they had the money to afford a beautiful house out in the open where animals run freely among the wild plants and the sky meets the mountains in the distance.

The moving van would be arriving at 6 am tomorrow and it would be a day of directing traffic thru the beach condo they called home. Their last day of picking up loose ends and being sure everything was done was coming to an end. The morning would come quickly and so they dressed together pulling from their closet what few things that were left to wear. In sweat suits t-shirts, hers in light blue his in black, they sat on the couch and gobbled up the Ty food Alex that had brought home. After the week of taping boxes and making last minute phone calls Alex and Jo were tired but the excitement of a new life had lit a bright fire in their hearts. "Let's go have this champaign and watch the sunset," Alex said as he pushed the corkscrew into his pants pocket and bunched a blanket under his arm.

With their hair still wet from their shower and bundled up in their hooded sweatshirts they walked out of the condo down the path to the beach with Dancer in tow all looking around knowing it would be some time before they returned. Their timing was perfect, though, as the last bit of sun was still out on the horizon and the day had given in to the coolness that comes as night falls. They opened the sparkling wine and sat together wrapped in blankets watching the sky. Side by side they began picking the names of their children. "Michelle, Scott and Amber" Joanna said.

"Michelle, Donald, and Mia" Alex replied.

"Oh, Mia I like that".

And while the sun was setting, the two lovers sat in quiet, knowing the trust of what life would come. The picture before them was like a painting, the one Joanna had dreamed of for so long and nothing could be more beautiful. There was no longing, no yearning, their love was committed and complete. quiet and peaceful were the sky, Joanna, Alex, and Dancer.

The End

About the Author

Wendy Ellis was raised in Upstate New York where sailing and boating on the Great Lakes was the highlight of summer activities. Later, attending the University of Arizona she went on to become a nurse although her professors said writing seems to be what you do best. As a NICU nurse in a large hospital, her every day was filled with many people. Nurses, patients, parents and medical staff all touched her life with their stories of struggle and triumph. She began to write their stories to share those wonderful moments when everything you thought you knew was right suddenly went wrong and then somehow came around full circle. "You need to remember the best times and how you got there," she says.

Escaping the Arizona summer heat she vacations in California and Florida, and winter trips are to the Caribbean or Colorado and Canada to enjoy skiing and a white Christmas. Skiing with the FWSA she has earned several medals. Having a love for animals she raised Labrador retrievers who were adopted by her new friends and colleagues. Interested in art and healing she is a published photographer, painter and Reiki Master.

Wendy has been published in an educational journal in the U.S. and England.

If you loved this book then, look for New Releases by Wendy Ellis Coming Soon!

If you enjoyed this book, I would love it if you would help others enjoy it as well. LEND it, RECOMMEND it, or REVIEW it. The greatest gift you can give an author is to spread the word to others.

Visit the Wendy Ellis website at
www.wendyellisbooks.com

Contact Wendy at wendyellisbooks@gmail.com

www.ingramcontent.com/pod-product-compliance
Lightning Source LLC
Chambersburg PA
CBHW060917180626
46817CB00004B/1291